AVALA IS FALLING

T0324450

OTHER TITLES IN THE SERIES

On the cover: Milena Pavlović-Barili, *Hot Pink with Cool Grey,* illustration published in *Vogue* on January 15th, 1940.

AVALA IS FALLING

Biljana Jovanović

Translated by *John K. Cox*

Central European University Press

Budapest • New York

Published in 2020 by

Central European University Press

Nádor utca 9, H-1051 Budapest, Hungary
Tel: +36-1-327-3138 or 327-3000
E-mail: ceupress@press.ceu.edu
Website: www.ceupress.com

400 West 59th Street, New York NY 10019, USA

Translation of this book is supported by the Ministry of Culture and Media of the
Republic of Serbia.

Република Србија
Министарство културе и информисања

ISBN 978-963-386-357-2
ISSN 1418-0162

Library of Congress Control Number: 2020937253

Printed in Hungary by
Prime Rate Kft., Budapest

Contents

Translator's Preface

It is an honor to have had this chance to translate a second novel by Biljana Jovanović, an author whose work, ideas, and ideals I greatly admire. There is more to her, from her, and more from the broadening Serbian and Yugoslav canon she exemplifies. I am very grateful to Rastko Močnik for making this project possible and for generously providing background material.

The source volume for this translation is: Biljana Jovanović, *Pada Avala*. Beograd: Nezavisna izdanje, 1981.

Jovanović's style in this novel is challenging. *Avant-garde* writers are most interesting, in my view, when their ideas keep pace with their departures from received forms, so I hope that readers of this translation will not mind having to process certain irregularities of punctuation, spacing, diction, etc., in this text. They were the author's intent, and they are part of an innovative aesthetic and part of an important message.

Since this is the most difficult book, in terms of its language, that I have ever translated, my list of debts for linguistic help is even longer than usual. I sincerely hope these folks know how much I appreciate their generous support with words and encouragement. I translate novels like this because I love them as art and because I am pretty much obsessed with finding different ways to understand recent life in Yugoslavia, or, shall we say, Serbia and the Balkans and Danubia. The presence of people like the ones in this list means that art and scholarship like this are both worthwhile and ... possible. I'd like to give a big shout out to: Patrick Apić, Tamara Vujanić Apić, Muharem Bazdulj, Milan Bogdanović, Kathleen Turley Cox, Biljana Dojčinović, Jovana Đurović, THE Jeff Johnson, Jasmina Lukić, Tijana Matijević, Dragan Miljković, Ivan Nador, Marijana Nedeljković, Aleksandar Štulhofer, Ajla Terzić, and Dennis Vulović.

This volume, along with my previous translation of Jovanović's *Dogs and Others* (Istros Press), was underwritten in part by cultural funds from the Ministry of Culture and Media of the Republic of Serbia, and I gratefully acknowledge this assistance.

This translation is dedicated to Dušan Bogdanović (aka KK4), who has never ceased to amaze me with his enthusiastic knowledge of etymology, philology, dialects, and the most far-flung fields of diction, from Turkicisms to urban slang. Over the years he has taught me more Serbian than anyone else on the planet, introduced me to all kinds of good people, arranged the purchase of a lot of great books, and sharpened my thinking on historical, political, and cultural (oh yes, and gastronomic!) issues. Thanks, Duško!

John K. Cox

The biographer of Jelena Belovuk, in the manner of all pedantic and responsible biographers, has taken down everything that the flutist Belovuk said to him over the course of their friendship. It is necessary to add here that Jelena's biographer, although he participated in her life, but of course not in the same way as Jelena herself, was unable to avoid arbitrariness and contradictions, as well as lies.

B. J.

CHAPTER ONE

Introductory Remarks by Jelena's Biographer

What an assignment! Above all, to record. All handbooks worthy of their salt and intended for those who compile biographies of famous people mention: date of birth, position of the stars, family origins, connections to their surroundings, and telepathic proclivities. I feel that the efforts of people who construct the fame of others are similar to the work of mice and moles; circular burrowing through the earth—canals, precise organization, carefully sealed holes—hiding places. The main thing in this entire enterprise, which is nonetheless less barren than I myself am, is that one should try to establish the relationship of Jelena Belovuk to Jelena Belovuk; and the relationship of Jelena Belovuk to what isn't Jelena Belovuk. Above all, dig a hole, prepare the edges of it well, and then probe the interior structure!

It's necessary for us to employ the same procedure from the other end, too! To wit: before beginning to form judgments about Jelena Belovuk, throw out all your assumptions about her body or her mind. Investigate all of the feelings that could be both love and hatred, including in her person (as if the point here were a general revision of your possibilities) and investigate

1

yourself! That is, look into yourself in Jelena Belovuk; and check yourself over against Jelena Belovuk.

Only then will it be allowed for you to wonder:

Who is Jelena Belovuk?

Who are the parents of Jelena Belovuk?

Is Jelena Belovuk's lover an influential person?

What does this Jelena Belovuk really want?

Where is Jelena Belovuk?

And now, really concretely:

My precision is the precision of a watch-maker; but what follows is the vaguest of nonsense, fabrication, falsehood, whispering behind people's backs and along their backs, along the spine, so to speak, about Jelena Belovuk, the least precise woman in existence on the planet! One has to keep in mind, like money in one's pocket, just one little thing: that my responsibility in this regard is void; events are more than truthful; I bear none of the blame for that.

CHAPTER TWO

Mr. Swede, the Moustache

The telephone conversation between Mr. Swede the Mustache and me on the last Saturday in June proceeded in this manner:

"This is Jelena."

"Well … go on!"

"Is that you, Swede?"

"It is. What's up?"

"Hey Swede, this is your good-for-nothing hopeless Lenka!"

The Swede was silent for a moment, and then let out a really loud breath (furiously) and cleared his throat!

"Are we going to see each other?" (I ask him.)

"No."

"Why?"

"You said … you Swedish bum … that I should get in touch with you."

"I said that by accident." The Swede was blushing for sure, starting to wheeze, and sweating, until out of his mouth tumbled, coldly Swedishly:

"I'm in a hurry. Bye."

He broke off the conversation without waiting for me to tell him goodbye. You Swedish red-haired mustachioed fart-face you're gonna pay for this … I was at a loss for three minutes. In minute four I lit up a cigarette. I smoke it for exactly five minutes. Five minutes, too, for me to put on that dress with the cut-out shaped like a rhomboid at the spot that's kind of like the middle of your spinal column. Sheer black tights, made by Polzela, (the only ones that stuck to your legs, from your toes to your belly button or a bit higher than your belly button, like a second skin, dark and smooth). I put on my clumpy yellow clogs (the Swede's gift from Sweden). Yellow and black on me—it could be an antithesis—the composition of colors on my body—intended for the outside world, for men but for the Swedish man most of all. When the colors are disassembled, for the interior world—for this room and for me, not even a thesis is left. I ask Hegel in passing: what can an antithesis mean if no thesis exists … I'm thinking of the colors (yellow and black) … Whatever the cost I want to be conspicuous and likable, this rhomboid-shaped cut-out, like a magical guillotine, will take off the Swede's big head, and then a light touch of my hand on the vertebrae in my rhomboidal opening, the press of a button, and his head will roll off, like a deflated basketball, right down by my feet, and then a little, just a touch, of soccer skill and: the Swede's head takes off, flies across Belgrade, subsequently to tumble into the Sava … There by the old bridge … it floats, collides with tugboats and some silly little ships … the traffic on all the bridges stops …

Ten minutes have now gone by since the conversation; I'm already on the stairs; I flick the cockroaches away with my foot, trying not to squish a single one of them, for the sound of the crackling, the exploding, of their gleaming armor (and out spill their milky yellow guts under the Swede's shoes, almost always) provokes my diaphragm into heaving up my bloated stomach and makes me burp, like when mirrors break or remain uncovered in the bathroom or on the table (all told there are three of them).

On the street, directly opposite the long powdered nose of the newspaper-stand lady (it's always/her nose/outside the protective glass), I hail a cab. I'm clumsy when I get in, first with one leg and then the other; is any other way even possible?

Am I a woman who is anxious for love? The sentence that is affirmative and inquiring at the same time passes (like a tiny bullet) through my head and that of the scowling driver. The driver's face was of course home to a mustache; out of the corner of my eye I could have checked that, to peer past his ears, but there was zero need for that. I was completely sure that the driver's face was scowling and mustachioed.

It is possible, taking me in with a cursory but almost exhaustive look-see, that the driver (convincingly) is expressing in three ways his thoughts about the relationship "love = me (Jelena Belovuk)": 1) Is this crazy woman eager for love? 2) This crazy woman desires the red-headed Swede! The third way is just a simplified version of the second: wacked-out Lenče has on her back a rhomboidal opening, the perfect Swede-trap.

That's how my cabbie and I were thinking, as we sat there with our eyes fixed on the column of cars in front of us. And then of course I asked him:

5

"Huh? ... Swede-trap ... What do you mean ... Explain!" And the taxi driver? He tilted his head a few degrees, barely enough to be able to see my cheeks, but enough to remember the red concentric circles on them. And that crazy cabbie then, with his tongue like a little vacuum cleaner, pulls out a piece (probably a big one) of food from between his teeth and, angry all of a sudden, says:

"You're carsick! What can I do, I mean, I can't let my window down. It's the draft, you know ... Is the smoke from my cigarette bothering you? I see I see it going into your face into your nostrils ... but what can I do, when I feel like smoking? Could you maybe open your window!"

Of course I was nauseous, but I didn't even think about opening the window; my head was spinning and my stomach was churning. If the trip lasted much longer, I was going to throw up my entire breakfast onto the back of his neck.

At the main post office, as if I were jumping into the water hugging my knees, I leapt out of the taxi. Then I leaned over towards the driver and saw: his mustache resembled the Swede's a great deal; in my most serious voice, I think it was a bit of a formal one, even, I informed him that I'd get money from my bank account there and bring it to him right away. He parked on the sidewalk right underneath the white signs: EXIT ENTRANCE.

But of course there did not exist a single little thing from the world of spirit and substance within the boundaries of good upbringing and behavior by which could be explained my abrupt decision to the cab driver with the Swede's mustache and a vacuum cleaner instead of a tongue and a fear of drafts—my decision not to pay for the ride. I had the money in my purse; there was nothing I needed to take care of at the post office. However, indefinite, completely unframed (just like the Swede's shaven head, naked; just like the Swede's face-unface, up close, distorted, flattened—the consequences of a past as a hooligan) was my belief in palingenesis. Swede, the red-headed bully and jerk that he was, the pace-setter among scoundrels, called me, for that reason: "the Jelena bitch, the front-runner among fools from Bežanijska."

I stayed in the post-office for about twenty minutes; I switched from the first line to the second, and then the third … At every counter I inquired about something different, and at each wicket the nervous female clerk directed me to one next door: Go to number 2 … 3 … 4 … 6 … and right down the line.

I skillfully abandoned my taxi driver, who waited patiently there the entire time, clicking his tongue-vacuum cleaner. I didn't run at all! All I did was walk past unnoticed (and despite the black-and-yellow rhombus, the destiny of the Swede, of men, adhering to the edges of that opening, to the little hairs on my skin) completely unnoticed … and less decisive, as a result …

Turning the corner (by the employees' entrance to the post office) I picked up the pace; I entered Tašmajdan Park and interrogated myself under my breath, holding up my first finger: 1) if all this stuff about palingenesis is true, and regardless of my man, Swedish, red-headed, the cabbie and I will meet in three thousand years, let's say, in the Madera or the Žagubica. By then I will have moved from a little plant into a high-energy blade of grass, for instance: cabbage—oh, right, well that's not a grass and maybe it's not all that caloric either, but no matter: from the cabbage into a spotted cow, and then I will as a thousand-year-old bullet fly into the Wanton Empress. Ha. And the cabbie? The cabbie would move from his mustache and that body into ivy, and then into an oak, my god, everything's there in palingenesis, nature itself, and then moving forward … after the oak tree … the taxi driver could … become for example … become … well, a man again hm why not? And the debt? We'll settle the debt like an empress and her mysterious roué, to the impetuous clicking of a tongue, in a location with firmly shut windows, because of the draft, obviously; with everyone hiccuping and frowning in equal parts.

I giggle; I graze against the little boys and girls, a bit roughly, in passing. I popped a big lanky rowdy on the side of the head because he slapped my ass. After that he pelted me with gravel from a distance with a slingshot. It's important for the taxi driver and me to update in our future life the relationship that now resides in the digits on the meter in his car: 4585. So, thanks to our future in the Madera and a new life, I just can't feel like a thief.

I exit Tašmajdan Park by the School of Mechanical Engineering and out of breath I get to the streetcar stop ahead of the streetcar: 2, 10. In streetcar #10, nobody noticed the secret signals from my body: yellow-black-rhomboid-skin totally white. I thought about how people had become vulgarians and all sorts of other stuff, and I chewed my lower lip angrily and tapped on my front teeth like dentists do with their little metallic mirror things.

At Karađorđe Park I bought 100g of sunflower seeds from grinning red-haired Ismar as I was getting out. (That grin is a crafty one.)

The streetcar with its tolling (it's a contemporary Notre Dame, sluggish, wobbly, and perpetually pregnant with Christ, corpulent and indescribably ugly) continues towards Voždovac, unsteadily I (I'm also a streetcar—a whole crowd of people is squatting in my stomach) clatter along in my clodhoppers in the opposite direction; I'm spitting out the little shells from the seeds, but some of them I chew up whole. Actually I do this with a lot of them, because I don't know how to break their belly-like bulges open from the top down; I'm devising revenge on the red-headed Swede.

At the corner of Ohrid Street, with the tracks and the mob, there's a grocery store. The window washer for this whole area is Swede the Mustache. He is fast and skilled at his job and he does his jobs with two other guys, both of them also former hoodlums. The Swede told me how the three of them sometimes tried to rape or did rape women and then showed them some papers, certificates of mental incompetence, legal unaccountability, and the like.

When I reached the grocery store, I stop, and like that—in an upright position—I'm pondering the most efficient modalities of vengeance: the sparkling clean glass windows of the grocery store I will smear with mud, wet earth, garbage (the remains of food, the kohlrabi-like eggs and the shells of roasted red paprika); I'll collect it all in rubbish bins, poking around through them to find the grossest garbage I can. The bins are located in the courtyard of Bldg. No. 7, three houses down from the grocery store on the left side. I was within an ace of hauling over an entire bin. What sentimentality! The Swede and I made love for the first time next to these bins on the vomit-stained concrete. There were a bunch of cats all around—they weren't being voyeurs, in contrast to people—their heads protruding from behind strung-up sheets and flower pots on the balconies; the cats strolled about atop the bins disinterestedly, past us, across the whole courtyard. There's no other building on Ohrid Street that has a courtyard like that one, with its ignoramus cats and balconies of resident voyeurs. And by the way I think that No. 7 is the only building to have a courtyard.

I was facing the woman who ran the flower stall on the street, and she decided, probably, that I had a mind to buy something, from her ... from that ... of hers. I stood so long between the shopping center and her ... I hesitated! Finally I gave up and concluded that it was dumb ... for now ... It was daytime then; when it's evening I'll ... tomorrow, the day after tomorrow ... No, I'll do it on Saturday, next Saturday, it would be best on Saturday, on that one ... on Saturdays the Swede washes windows ... and they cleaned them today, too. I leave the florist in doubt and with a hand and a red flower on offer; she yells "Oh c'mon. It's only three dinars!"

Mr. Swede, the Moustache

I slip on down the street. Along the way I see my reflection in the heart-shaped, conical, cubical, and rectangular mirrors, of all sizes, in the display cases at two glasscutters.' I ascertain, abruptly, that the opening (the rhomb on my spine) isn't all that big. It's almost inconspicuous. I catch sight of the huge bags under my eyes (I've never seen anything so gray) and two poles in my baggy black clothes. I look at the waiter from the Café Orač (we know each other, the Orač waiter and I) straight in the eye and I want right away at that very moment to light into him like a mad dog, but I only whisper: the world was not built on phalluses, on the vagina, or the fruits of sweat and cologne, or on the uterus, Mr. Sale (I'm using baby talk for the fat jackass), that's pure fiction, as is the stew, the worst mućkalica in the city, that you are toting right now. Sale (the waiter) is already two meters past me, and I'm still whispering to him, in a most familiar way, the fat Sale, as if to my own stomach: Salence, dear little Sale, the ignoramus cats are smarter than you, the voyeurs behind their checkered bedsheets are smarter than you, and so are the women who don't report the rape after seeing the falsified certificates of mental unaccountability for the Mustache and for his window-washing companions.

In streetcar no. 3, I finally resolve to take things into my own hands, things that are directly connected with my external appearance and with what that might mean.

I sat down; I don't look out through the smeared windows like usual. Instead I turn to face the interior of the streetcar. Since I am seated, the first things I see level with my eyes are two hands; their reddened wrists are resting on the metal tops of the seatbacks in front of me.

11

I know that the metal bars in all streetcars in all buses are greasy and gross … These two broad, ornamented, reliable hands must be sweating on the underside. Immediately adjacent to them, also at eye level, but a touch over to the right, I see two skirts, wrinkled and pleated, around groin level; a third, taut with concealed pleasure, touches the first two every time the streetcar shakes. I incline my eyes to the right and glimpse a notched zipper, held on tightly to a pair of jeans with firm stitching. The fertile packages are distinguishable by their part, their contoured stitching; the invisible phallus, emperor of the rustling bed, caesar of the vomit-covered concrete, above the trough urinals in public bathrooms; the heir to the throne, mounted, that is, on streetcar no. 3; the underage exiled child-emperor phallus! I snicker; the little sacks with their parts, balloons in women's dreams; tonight's successful or unsuccessful lover (the kingdom could be right underfoot) makes for the exit, most likely, for I lose him from view. In the streetcar the background noise means that no one paid any attention to my giggling.

I get off at the New Cemetery stop. In the "Kosovo Peony" café, I drink two herbal liqueurs, for my stomach, and then I leave in a somber mood; I remember that it's almost mandatory to fill a stomach (with food) when it is dry, grieving, and wrung out by romantic sorrows—the red-haired Swede tore his fate off my back with one stroke, efficiently, as pedantically as when he washes windows (he doesn't leave behind the smallest speck of dirt); he leaves no trace of it on my skin.

After nearly half an hour, with a feeling of disgust (at the "Peony" I'd eaten spoiled meat), there I am, yellow-clogging about, with yellowness, emptiness, boredom, and hoovered insides (I vomited in front of the doors to a florist's, where the clerks who were just cleaning up cursed at me); I kicked the foliage of their fake wreaths and the real ones, and I kicked little stones, and when I was all kicked out I entered a hairdresser's called "Dara."

"May I help you?"

"I'd like to have my hair … cut, and colored, and washed."

"Will do."

The hand of "Dara" pointed me to a chair behind a dirty purple-yellow curtain; I saw a sink above the chair, and a large mirror in front of it. I almost started crying; I clenched my fists, my jaw, and the muscles in my cheeks; I crossed and uncrossed and recrossed my legs and stared straight ahead with huge eyes; I pushed my head up between "Dara's" hands and into her sheet metal washbasin; when the stream of lukewarm water commenced its run across my temples, I said calmly: Jelena this is a very very important undertaking, the cutting and coloring, like a rite of cleansing.

My hair had been red, and all the way down to my shoulder blades (men's open eyes would turn and automatically dry my hair, better than a hair-dryer, like a centrifuge in a little heliomatic machine); now it was short, indescribably short and ineffably black. I looked like a tadpole. But, I think, I am almost convinced once and for all, like St. Basil with his healing powers, that with the hair I cut off my lust, Alp-sized, as big as the Šar Mountains, for the Swede, the red-headed Swede.

13

CHAPTER THREE

Mića, the Future Officer

Marijana, my accomplice in the first experiences of body and soul, doesn't believe a single word I say:

"Jelena, my white-wolved goatlet, white-harted rotten putrid udder"—hummed bug-eyed Mića around the house. "Our local Jelena, at 20 Masarikova St., has only one tit … Udders and tits have the same function … The differences are quite inconsequential for the lover."

"But Mića, why only one?"

Decked out in kitchen cloths, napkins, and towels, he said: You won't believe me, Marijana … if I say that the second one fell off because the gum arabic dried out, and also because gum arabic has been proven to be the worst adhesive ever. What happened to her other boob? My bug-eyed lover pointed to a little table with brass shackles, announcing that the second breast was wrapped up in tinfoil like the hand of St. Charalambos and that it's locked in the drawer.

I left his apartment with bruises and a bad cold; from that I have this neurodermatitis on my right cheek. It comes with Mića's passion. I'd bet you four pieces of marzipan each that you've never experienced anything like this: he pushed me under the dining room table, jumped on me like I was a yoga mat, leaned me against the edge of the metal bathtub as if I were a red-cratered sponge. The way that thing with the bathtub went down, by the way, I could've had my head cracked open at any moment.

Marijana giggles: "Like a dead cat or a cockroach smeared on the rim of the tub, ha ha ha … My *goood*, Jelena, couldn't he have … wrung you out … less than a sponge?"

Mića has huge hips and a huge head on a little body.

Marijana concludes: "His hips are big from all the fucking and his head is big because of his high IQ" (Marijana interprets everything literally). I tell her that the size of people's skulls has no connection with their IQ's. Things are actually the other way around: hips are big when you're intelligent, because brains run from your left and right eyes diagonally and intersect and go into the right and left hips, respectively, and the head is big on account of the macrocosmic quantities of semen that Mića, the future military officer, devotedly: in military style: sprays all over the terrace, the clean laundry, the yellow-green leaves of the *Dieffenbachia*, across the reddish brown leaves of that other plant, all over the linoleum, the door to the bathroom, the walls and the ceiling (when Officer Mića's salvos are not uniform but are nonetheless valiant, as when confronting a superior enemy).

I first met Mića at an exhibition of psychedelic art. Both of the rooms were packed with people, so that we found ourselves next to each other's folded knees (we were seated). We only managed to see the red color of the projection, spilling across that left third of the canvas, and the legs in brown and black shoes worn by the visitors who were standing all around and in front of us. Getting to know somebody when there's a concealed lust factor always starts with some kind of ambiguous dialogue, general position-taking, the ignition of untold numbers of cigarettes ... and through all of that, believe me, Marijana, Mića and I (we verified it later) pursed our lips till they ached, sniffled loudly, and pleated our foreheads until they looked like the Greek letter omega; during the projection, we burned our way through a mountain of smokes; we exhaled into each other's faces, in between the other visitors, through their legs, and then waved the smoke away with our hands, and every time we did so we touched each other and pretended it was an accident.

"Did both of you really have an omega on your forehead?" (Asked Marijana.)

We left the exhibition before it was over and headed for his house, in Masarikova Street. I stayed there for six days, wearing his threadbare coat. Mića requested I wear it and ... that I go barefoot for the whole six days. There was no carpet or any similar kind of padding or pallet in the room, and the foyer, kitchen, and bath had linoleum ... Just imagine, Marijana, he slept with me on the cold linoleum under the table in the foyer, next to the bathtub; he let down the blinds and turned off the light. He was shy, and he always avoided eye contact.

"I can't believe that a future officer wouldn't have a pair of slippers in his house!" (Said the ever so wise Marijana.)

It was boring, and above all tedious, this arousal of Mića's passion for variation; as a future military person he wanted to try out all battle positions, not shrinking from any dangers: glass on the floor, bugs under the table, cold, and the rest of it. Believe me, Marijana, the only thing that kept me in that apartment for six days was Mića's divine, pouty nose, with its big bulging birthmark on the tip. All of my lust, which troubled my otherwise clear eyes and my gaze, was contained in fact in the rubbing of Mića's nose with its marvelous birthmark over my left shoulder, and it was especially exciting under that table, in the foyer.

"What nonsense, Jelena … Why the left shoulder, exactly?" (Marijana was amazed.)

It's a matter of the asymmetrical arrangement of nerves and points sensitive to the touch of Mića's nose. Anyway, we also tried it with my right shoulder, and my belly button."

"Jelena, you're a skanky thing, getting it on with all that licking and rubbing under the table in the foyer, on the linoleum!" (Marijana said.)

Mića spent the rest of the time (what remained between the tub, the table, and the linoleum, and after it all). Studying world maps, convincing me that Greenland should be drawn a little to the left and down some. He maintained that the scale was off, and he discovered that Greenland is completely empty, and that you can get there quite easily from Iceland, across the Denmark Strait. There were here, Marijana, on the linoleum, strewn all over, many maps and some booklets about the oceans. And bug-eyed Mića was talking all sorts of rot. He said, for instance, that he could fashion, lickety-split, a Bay of St. Jelena, or a Gulf of St. George, out of his ancient, banged-up sheet metal bathtub. I can't remember which one it was, exactly. Using his clippers I cut my toenails and placed them on top of the maps, covering up the bays, straits, islands, and basically just the complete asininity of these expanses. I told him that traveling was a completely barbarous undertaking, and something else that I can't recall.

The next day I left. But that night, first, before going to bed but after the geography thing and the thing with my nail clippings, the divine Mića said to me, just like this: "Good night, Yelenskaya, the whitest woman of Greenland."

In the morning I bought fresh dahlias and hung them around the apartment, where it was feasible, with rubber bands holding them to jars and others tied up with some kitchen rags. The apartment resembled a Christmas tree, and my Mića, asleep on the pallet on the floor, looked like a holiday cake.

Before leaving, I wiped—carefully, believe me, Marijana—with a damp flannel cloth and some BIS cleaner all the surfaces that had come into contact with the brave future officer's semen. I bought two bags of marzipan at the pastry shop on Zmaj Jovina Street, crumbled one of the daffodils, mixed it with the marzipan, and put it into a little porcelain dish on the table in the foyer.

With more sagacity than she'd shown as long as we'd known each other, Marijana said: "You thought of everything!"

I took Marijana's arm as we crossed the street—at the worst intersection in town; the wind blew both of our skirts up (they were white, the skirts) and revealed Marijana's long legs and my somewhat shorter ones. We lit our cigarettes and entered the building. Outside the door, Marijana asked: "What else did he say to you?"

"Who?"

"Well, Mića!"

"He said: 'Blue eyes are analytical, green ones are for overachievers and bullies, black ones are poetic, and brown is for whores.'"

"He really talked to you like that?"

"Just like that. In the tub, while we were having a bath."

At that point Marijana stuck her key into the lock, flipped on the light in the hallway, and we went in, after first putting out our cigarettes on the concrete floor, and we called out our greetings to Marijana's aunt. It was her apartment.

CHAPTER FOUR

Propellers, Motors I

———

"Vladica, the photographer, is a real man."

"That doesn't mean much," says my companion, Marijana.

"Jelena, you are making groundless claims, based on what your little toe says all dwarfish and bent and miserable down there on your left leg, as if you had rheumatism and could predict the weather, rain, precipitation, storms, deep blue funks, and the like. One thinks syllogistically about men; they require logic as firm as their women's behinds, and not the intuition emanating from the little toe of your left foot, which is stunted anyway."

"All right," I say to her and think to myself how packed with malice she is, like the airport in Surčin with its planes in July. "Fine," I tell her, pacified and nearly convinced:

"Premise: from Year One of our era, the world has been ruled by people born in the sign of the fish."

Marijana listens attentively, but with an ironic smile on her lips.

"Premise: Vladica, the photographer (also known as The Caravel), was born in the sign of the fish."

Marijana's restraining herself; she's about to burst out laughing, the spasm just washes out over her face the way an airplane rolls along its runway, and takes off. Marijana pushes over her seat, that is, the backrest of her seat and explodes with laughter like a nylon stocking.

"The conclusion is: Vladica, the photographer, is a real man, that is, a man—a hypothetical ruler."

"Maybe that's a syllogism and not a valid deduction," I said in justification, or apology, to the accursed temptress.

"But Vladica, a.k.a. The Caravel, has little hairs coming out of his nose, and with long-term training they could take the shape of a fish-head."

Marijana shrieks and asks, full of herself: "Can any other part of him take the shape of a fish?"

"Not necessary, Marijana. Vladica has a fish tattoo, actually it's two fish, swimming in opposite directions, exactly like on the zodiac symbol, on his calf, the back of his hands, and his Adam's apple."

At the mention of his Adam's apple, Marijana put on a serious face again. She was always deadly earnest when she encountered symbols having to do with religion, paradise, or masculinity. She was enchanted by dumbass things: men's necks, the Garden of Eden, the curse of the apple, and man's compassion on that occasion.

"Last Thursday I was wearing my Adidas running shoes and a checkered shawl wound snugly around my neck; the ends of it were dragging along the ground. I was determined to die like Duncan."

Marijana says: "Don't lie, Jelče. You wrapped that shawl around your neck because of your angina, bronchitis, and the other trivial things that have beset you. Not because of Isadora."

"Vladica, the photographer, takes pictures of propellers, motors, airplane wings, cockpits, and letters: JAT; other letters: DC9; other letters: CARAVEL."

Marijana, like the utter illiterate that she is: "Hence his own nickname, surely 'coz he plans on attaching it to his dick as advertising."

Marijana is vulgar. She asks: "What else does Vladica the photographer, a real man, take pictures of?"

He photographs with the greatest possible care (he checks the opening of the diaphragm shutter several times, the light, distance) the stewardesses' asses, pilots, and the dreams, displayed on their faces, of life that begins when one is 50, gadgets, parallel bars, mechanical labor-saving devices, stationary bikes, weight sets—for the maintenance of life, which starts, brooking no delay, in year fifty; the pilots schlep them (home from distant journeys) through the halls of the airport, and the customs officials go easy on life at fifty.

And Marijana: "You're making stuff up again, Jelče."

"Imagine, on Thursday he went up to a stewardess, before he took the portrait of her back and her backside, lifted her skirt, saying: 'Okay ma'am, or miss, where's that little pussy of yours where does the (young?) lady keep the womanly charms she's smuggling—it's for the audio-video test for stewardesses?' The flight attendant let out a full-throated shriek and clobbered him with an airplane-sized slap to the face."

Marijana: "Caravel bowled over by a Boeingess."

In order to avenge himself on the airport staff, Vladica ran out unnoticed onto the runway and climbed up on the wing of the plane, shouting: "What women!

You pilots, my comrades and friends! The airplane is better—you fly it and you get excited—you fear it and you're happy about it."

Marijana then, earnestly: "Exactly. Vladica is right. Comrade pilots test out every one of the psychic phases."

After that he climbed up into the cabin, unobserved—they thought he was one of the workers or from the cleaning crew; I was hanging out on the airport's observation deck and just in case standing guard including keeping watch on my own fear. In truth there were some workers, electricians and what-not, hanging around the plane, which incidentally had just landed."

Marijana moronically once more: "What happened to the passengers?"

"You know, Marijana, that thing that Vladica the photographer said about the two of us, that we were thinly shadowed, in the photographic sense, which means, translated into our language: while we stand around grinning, baring our teeth, hands on our hips, we make narrow shadows; he said the same thing or something similar about the airplane he was climbing around on."

Marijana said, shaking her head and her artificial eyelashes: "I don't understand any of this."

Understanding's not necessary for thing, events, that don't have a firm empirical foundation or, let's say that are not a priori established. Therefore, from Marijana's cerebral position (history tells us that that position is inviolable) these things, these events, are nonsensical; in point of fact they are not worthy of our cognition and possible confirmation.

"Vladica the photographer and I, following his alpinistic and photographic projects, had a seat in the airport restaurant and drank that famous airport coffee and talked trash."

Marijana, very much interested: "About whom, Jelče?"

"Not you, Marijana. I told you already that as far as both you and I are concerned, Vladica expressed his praise, saying that we are thin-shadowed. We were talking about Mirča, that hooligan from Novi Beograd, made in Italy, Mirča's blue eyes, unbuttoned shirt, about Mirča's butt-made in Italy, about his bovine eyelashes and his Dorćol way of walking. Then we had a Coca-Cola. Vladica, after his Coke, belched loudly, super loud. We kept on and on sitting there till the last plane had landed. When the boy passengers and the girl passengers came down the corridor and alongside us, Vladica pulled a pocket mirror out of my purse and caught with it: shadows, bulges, white lines, fulnesses, slits, carryon-on bags, droopy ears, and other stuff above, below, and around women's skirts. We rode back together on the JAT bus with the boy passengers and the girl passengers. In the bus, Vladica the photographer did the same thing with the mirror. He said it was a technique of modern photography, more effective than most. I didn't doubt it."

Marijana then picked up the astrological column, from her Los Angeles Times; the sections about the fish, the scorpion, the water-pourer, and the archer were translated by our mutual acquaintance Mirča, also known as Made in Italy. The prophecies were from 1952.

But that doesn't matter in the least, for horoscope truths are for the most part valid for at least five decades calculated from the year in which they were composed. That means that Marijana and I can goggle at the horoscopes with confidence until the year 2000, and two years beyond. It's especially important that astrological personages across the ocean are the ones compiling the horoscopes.

Marijana read, for Aquarius—both of us were under that sign:

You feel dynamic, predestined to fulfill your plans at any cost.

We considered everything (along with the rest of the text, which it would be a drag to reproduce here) as was appropriate. Everyone knows what their type of appropriate understanding is. Then we dialed a number on the phone jointly (Vladica's) and cordially invited him to come interpret a few words in the prediction that were unfamiliar to us.

We made coffee for him (together: Marijana put water and sugar in the Turkish coffee pot and I added the coffee, we filled glasses with Coca-Cola, although he used to burp too loud. As loud as could be.

CHAPTER FIVE

Marijana Says:
"There's a Daffodil Between My Legs"

Marijana and I leave together, when we're sleepy, in our rolled-down socks, on our long legs, every morning, for the Academy. Recently we went in on a rented apartment together. In that place piled up: men, newspapers, musical notes, music monographs, panty hose, and jars of yogurt. Marijana was in the piano department; when she played, she resembled a man in everything she did. I played the flute, using my pretty lips and my swollen knotty fingers.

We return to our mutual quarters at differing times, on the 13th floor on Milaševa Street, with the deep and sincere yearning to bring men, newspapers, musical notes, our stories, and the socks, and the underwear drying on the radiators into some kind of order, hierarchical, at last. It was a must for us to classify the above-mentioned items according to: 1) their overall significance for apartment 128; 2) their purpose and the suitability of that purpose; and 3) length of use.

We lived together for a year. One day Marijana simply ran away, leaving me with the unpaid bills: the rent, the deposit and bills for the apartment, telephone, water, heating, electricity, and yoghurt. On that day, she came back from the Academy earlier than usual. As soon as she hit the door she started crying out, full of emotion: "Jelena, Jelena, there's a daffodil between my legs … from my walks, from having flat feet, from the eroticism in my ankles and a little above there, you understand; there's nothing strange here; it all hurts, I feel them, Jelekče (an example of her baby-talk to me), and there's no physical touching in any of it; you sleep with a man and touching doesn't exist; my nonexistent chance, therefore, to survive as a woman; a touch … pelvises are unhinged … you give birth to a tongue-tied child and once more no touch exists … not then either … when the baby comes out … Nothing, but a whole lot of nothing about this is out of the ordinary … but it's simple. You know what I mean, like Padre Antonio Soler … exactly like that."

She removed her make-up; she doused cotton deep into a little pot of "cleansing," without ceasing to speak. We did not take a break—over coffee and cigarettes—from the conversation. And also it wasn't a conversation. It was "from talk" and "under talk." (Those were Marijana's terms.) Then Marijana undressed, hung up her clothes (the red wool dress) on the brass handle on the bathroom door; she did not close the door; while she showered, she dropped the soap several times. She rattled on and on, that Marijana, damn her. She talked about how she could fall in love at any minute with long legs (a man's) thick necks (men's) tumescent zippers (men's), big strong biceps, shoulders grown broad enough for two beds at the same time (men's). Of lips, eyes, eyelashes, forehead, and nose, there was no talk;

Marijana says that the faces of men are garden-variety fabrications, inaccuracies, and thus unimportant.

After that, she put on a different dress, re-did her make-up, applying a whole 20 g. of foundation; she assembled a portion of the collective inventory of the stuff strewn all over the apartment, took all the sheet music (including mine), musicology books, kissed me on the forehead, the cheek (one), my neck and my nose, and scampered out; Marijana ran out, hopping aggressively down the steps two at a time, and out into the street.

I comprehended everything! Furious and sour at her departure, I just gave a dismissive wave of my hand and decided right then and there to wash the windows. Ha! Physical labor to reign in the emotions—the well-intentioned advice of all the people who spend time with me.

Subsequently: I make notes on paper that has lines, dots, and circles—for changes in altitude; I note changes in my vitality expressed in the smallest metric units—millimeters; because Marijana left, because of the washed windows, because of the birth of a child. A millimetric plan for the compression of ideas into pores, a little square of skin, a piece of my tongue, filling my entire trap; everything incorporeal.

Enter strictly and precisely every fraction of a millimeter. That's how you will best know how much your child has grown. How much it has surpassed you—its parents—and your parents, your grandfathers and grandmothers; and via the grandpas and grandmas you will know by how much it exceeds your ancestors. If you conscientiously note down every little change in the growth of your one and only, you will see: a generation of six-and-a-half footers is coming; you are not tall, and your parents are tiny, compared to your one child, unforeseeably … tiny. Have some respect for this unavoidable growth of the generations; with height increases also resistance to treacherous viruses, bacteria of every sort, and all times of spiritual ailments!

Vitality at the zero mark

30 … cm from the floor—the distance of the graph attached to the wall with a yellowish tack and the first shoelace of your one and only (from one of the shoes he was wearing the day he first walked), be precise, exactly 30 cm off the floor, that is, from the last little line of the graphic. The only child has to exceed, and this is obligatory, its creators and pre-creators and progenitors!

It is imperative: I will sleep 14 hours per day; I could sleep for all twenty-four; I will unplug the telephone; I'll turn the lock in the door several times (this is totally possible); I shall close the windows (dirty air is harmful for my one and only); I'll lower the blinds as far as I can without making the room altogether dark; I will empty my stomach, my bowels, my mouth ready for lust and the claptrap that comes together with lust, with an enema, with bitter salts and similar effective purgatives (the only child must have a clean space in which to grow). And then, train tickets, bus tickets, truck driver details and receipts, photos, hotel invoices, expressions of love, petitions of residents to the administration that they halt the cremations, at least for a while, during the summer months, for the tenants are unable to sleep, eat, or urinate, or sweat and squirm atop their legitimate wives on account of the overpowering fragrance, that is to say all the chaff from the list of documentation of a personal, that is, city, life, I will donate to the tenants' councilor, some local organization, or to Đorđe the philatelist, or something like that!

I will not, however, sleep with men under any circumstances.

But soon I can tell that this is getting me nowhere. My intentions are sincere, the labor enormous, but nonetheless success eludes me. It's paradoxical but true. All I did was: I cocked my head back so I could put some drops of "Benil" in my congested nose. That's all the adventure there was. The most forceful fact here is since Marijana's departure I have a perpetually stuffy nose.

I stood at the window; I called out to the neighbor, Bosa.

I stuck my hands way down into my pockets; no doubt, that is the uncertain position of a statue-body. I pace clumsily around the room, sluggishly as if blood is flowing out of my veins, across my shoes, and under the shoes, over the parquet floor, along the wall, out the window into Bosa's apartment next door, out of her apartment into the corridor, and then sloshing (blood wears moccasins) goes down all twelve floors, step by step, past the mailboxes on the ground floor, and stops on the sidewalk in front of the entrance-way; it all flows into the pocket of the philatelist, Đorđe, where it collects and then with an acrobat's leap, out of his pocket it goes … hopla, onto his lower lip (thin).

I scream through the window: "Booosa … It's me. I'm coming!"

Our neighbor Bosa did for Marijana and me the following good deed: paid all our bills during our absences; when we were gone, also, she received verbal messages for us, flowers, boxes of candy, unsealed threatening letters with curses on the margins—all from our visitors: who were desirers, high-grade and low-grade paranoiacs, men with broad backs and strapping third legs, and other masculine beauties. It so happened that she then asked them in for rakija, strudel, and coffee.

Our one-in-a-million neighbor, Bosa, sometimes, placed on their shoulders her boiling, advanced years, or on their stomachs, or on their broad and hairy calves; she put year after year into their ignorant mouths, after the strudel, rakija, and coffee. To this day Bosa subsists only on strudel washed down with rakija and coffee.

I zoom into her apartment, like a nervous yippy dog; Bosa—a "twelfth-floorer"—has already put the red-dotted coffee pot on the stove. She takes out fifty little pieces of strudel (I think that's how many there were) and placed a mega-bottle of rakija on the table.

Neighbor Bosa has yellow eyelashes, a bit of a yellowish mustache, and yellow yellow hair. Everything is more or less yellow. Conclusion (premature, you will say): Bosa is a completely correct woman; whatever she's doing can be watched readily, through her open windows without any drapes, from the neighboring apartment bloc, or from the corridor through the half-open door of her apartment. All of it through the eyes (of course) and ears of the 680 residents of our common praying mantis of a building on Milaševa Street. All that by way of … Bosa's uprightness. And everything being based on the assumption that Bosa's yellowness necessarily implies gentleness and kindness (680 tenants, curious, totally in harmony with Greek wisdom: I swear it's true—they ask: Does Bosa's carpet match the yellow drapes? If it does, her scrupulousness is complete; insofar as she is not also yellow between her legs, then remember: deceitfulness is not a part of this). Indeed, with fraud the goal could be achieved, that is, Bosa's yellowness. ENTIRE. It is apparently obvious that the six hundred and eighty Milaševa Street residents are disinclined to sophistic rashness and cunning.

While we drank coffee and gulped down our strudel and local hooch, a little bit of each, mixing it up, Bosa pierced my ears and I didn't feel a thing. On the little hanging part of her left ear, Bosa has a tattoo of a rose. It's a historical fact from the life of this little lady. I asked her who did it; it's so skillful, and I said that this rose of hers probably even smelled like something sweet; to tell the truth, it actually looked more like a clove, but no matter, a flower is a flower, even if it's a tattoo, on Bosa's left ear. Bosa told me something, at times swallowing her words simultaneously with large pieces of the strudel; the tattooed neighbor said that the little flower was a souvenir, of the simplest kind imaginable, more durable than any other drawing, and that it was utterly unimportant who did the memorializing on her left ear (on that separate lobe part), and it was particularly unimportant for me. She said it this way: "How does this concern you, sweetheart?"

Since Marijana failed to return to our shared apartment on the street with the monastery's name, I go out daily, before and after the conservatory, to Neighbor Bosa's; she was also known as "abbess of the 12th floor"; I drank rakija with her, and coffee, and talked about this and that for a long time, and plowed through strudel. In addition, one fact more, despite my vanity; I must communicate this clearly: since Marijana ran out of the highrise on Milaševa, not a single male individual has turned up at the door of apartment 128.

It's a trick of Marijana's, no doubt!

But, exactly five days and one-half of a sixth day after she left, I had a dream and I think it was something like this:

She comes back; I see her in the unwashed window; she comes in, and with the back of her hand tosses bald doves into the room; she's joyful. Marijana is joyful out of all proportion. She's here, in this room, the same as I am. Actually only Marijana and her hairless handy dorsal pigeons are present; I am not; only women know how to convince like that. She undresses again (the red wool dress once more); she strews her clothes about. Her undergarments slide snakelike from her body. Oh God, a female body naked in front of another woman's body. The problem is certainly not in the marvel of same-sexedness.

Marijana is beautiful. Incomprehensibly attractive. But, then, Marijana's mother was named Evgenija, her grandmother Natalija, and her great-grandmother Simonida. Do you get the significance and signification of these names for the female body? Just imagine how, by dint of names such as these, for example: Natalija's breasts could get bigger, and her forehead, her eyes. She could become a heavyset woman in general. Marijana's body grows through her ancestors, and the more names there are like theirs in her past, the more powerful, enduring, and Simonidian is her body.

The last time I dreamed about Marijana, she was on my shoulders; she slid down my cheeks, tickled my armpits; an enormous Marijana, a tangled ball, she rolls down the needle-like rough spots on my skin.

With her mute bald pigeons she went out through the window. Marijana, Natalija, Evegenija, fledgling girl-bird, seductress ….

None of the desired men knocked on the door of apartment 128. A refined and nasty trick by Marijana. Well, and Evgenija, and … maybe Natalija too?

CHAPTER SIX

Bautista Van Šoven
(Bautista Van Schouwen)[1,2]

T he man who was sitting at the end of the park by the Yugoslav Drama Theater could have been the Chilean, Bautista, to judge on the basis of his external distinguishing features: oval face, uneven haircut—longish in the front, dark; the plunging, symmetrical sideburns; the nose bent but regular; wide nostrils; with a thick unibrow filling the space between his forehead and nose—most unusual-looking. Bautista's right arm rested (bent at the elbow) on the shattered backrest of the bench; his fingers were lightly touching his brow—for the most part, this is exactly how Bautista sat. In his other hand (from this distance it looks to be painted dark blue) the man who resembled Bautista holds an unlit cigarette (the way I myself do it) in an

---

[1] The thirty-year old doctor Batista van Schouwen, member of the political committee of the MIR movement, was arrested in 1973 and subjected to cruel torture; later transferred to a military hospital in Valparaiso; in February of '75 a photograph of Bautista, suffering and abused but still alive, was taken in secret. The last news we have about him is that a lobotomy was performed on Bautista in the junta's hospital in Valparaiso.

[2] 1979, 1980, 1981—and currently: Bautista van Schouwen is probably no longer among the living.

awkward way—between his middle and fourth fingers. On his lips (I believe that I see) a crooked smile, but it could also be a wince—a dark edge—a line of desire on the lips makes the same shadows—an unfinished arc, bent the same way in a spasm as in a smile, on people's lips, in Chile.

From all of this it still isn't possible to conclude that the figure of the person on the bench, at one end of the park, is the figure of a thirty-year old man! However, Bautista's appearance has also deceived his pursuers, the police and women who came after him in groups.

Viewed differently—I approach the bench flamboyantly if unsteadily—his physique took on more importance: the way his eyebrows met like that was an indication of energy; while the shadow across his left cheek from the base of his nose to its tip was a reflection of mysteriousness—although it was a bit of physical regularity; but with Bautista the solid shadow on his cheek is surely (as if this were me, with a stationary bluegrayness on my face, hands, across my stomach, inside my head, inside my belly) the result of life and amour launched by surprise, in ambushes, in hallways sometimes and in secret living quarters in well-appointed buildings.

Now I am barely one step away from Bautista's unmoving body. My purse has slipped off of my shoulder; I wave it around like the clapper of a bell—I make it go in uniform orbits; one amplitude—pure lust from me through the pocketbook touches Bautista's clenched knees. I observe him: he has attractive lips, maybe a touch longer and curvier than mine; I can see a faint scar, looking like it's drawn on, coarse, from the edge of his beard over the underside of his chin to his Adam's apple.

"Can I sit here?" I asked him; and without waiting for an answer I put my purse down by his feet and had a seat, so close to him that all it would take was a single movement of my head and my lips would have found themselves on his cheek ... his firm cheek ... and then with just a twist they would skid over onto his mouth.

In this position I could see his scar clearly; it looked like a cut from a knife; red; somehow more like purple! Maybe they used hot tongs to leave tracks on him, their sign ... to what end, for what kind of evidence?

I asked him: "Did they try to kill you?"

"No, they didn't ... You know, the scar ... it's from a pruning knife ... in the village ... you know, back in the village!"

Bautista grinned; he moved his head away a little and let down his arm ... He appeared to have caught on to my intentions. From our new positions, Bautista could observe me ... But he didn't do it! He looked off to the side somewhere, dejected, from under his lowering eyebrows, and smoked his cigarette.

There can be no doubt that Van Schouwen escaped Valaparaiso, fled from that prison hospital, banged up as he was, bruised, swollen, half-dead; it was probably during his escape, when he was running, that he fell against the barbed wire strung around the walls of the prison hospital, and that's what pierced his neck, without touching that knot of life—his Adam's apple. I noticed that his neck was covered with sharp, stiff beard, but the scar was uncovered and, what's more, his face was smooth, shaved clean.

"Did you trip and fall? I ask him, and while doing so I deliberately touch one of his knees, the knee that seems broken—branched and thorny. Bautista moves to the edge of the bench, my hand slides unexpectedly from his knee, and my little finger, like a long, bent fish-hook, was left hanging on the fabric of his pants—a possibility that contact could be established, gently and noiselessly, by subterfuge.

Bautista raised his right arm again, and leaned his twisted torso firmly on his planted left hand. He turned his face to mine (of course that's completely the result of my strategy); his eyes, like two bloodthirsty black beasties, rushed in the direction of my stomach, the lower part of my stomach, and plunged down (skated along on) my left leg, grazing the side of my shoe, its rubber soul, the ground ... and it loitered for a few seconds on the purse that lay turned on its side close to his legs. (What did you expect? The slide of his corneas was provided for in my project!)

He snarled: "No, they were forcing me to finish my work before dusk; and in the rush, with me being so terribly worn out and agitated, this ... accident happened to me."

"So that means ... They didn't chase you? Go flying after you like the Furies? Weren't there bullets, dogs, guards, daggers, rapiers, all kinds of people?"

"I ran as if my life depended on it ... Exactly as if they were chasing me!"

"Maybe you saw Ricardo ... or Jorge? They must've been somewhere. Behind you ... I think they also escaped from ... Valparaiso?!?"

Not startled in the least by my curiosity, which otherwise, in other circumstances, could have been interpreted as ill-breeding, Bautista declaimed in an ironic voice:

"I lost my head while I was running, and your face came to me in a vision ... and heaven and earth had transformed into amplified interlocking pulsations and heartbeats ... And I saw you! As far as I can recall there was you, and nothing but you, before my eyes ... but ... Ricardo ... and someone named Jorge ... I didn't ... didn't see them anywhere!"

I had again dropped my hand onto his knee (that was, of course, part of the plan); as tenderly as I could I drew it up towards Bautista's crotch, keeping an earnest, calm look on my face, enthralled, for real, by the wonders of his escape, and trying to imagine the equally attractive faces of Jorge and Ricardo, who did not make it this far—to this bench at the end of the park by the Yugoslav Drama Theater. I felt under my fingers the hard wool of his sweater, and then his shirt, which was unbuttoned down to the middle of his chest; I fingered a button.

I looked at his profile and asked, pitifully:

"Did it hurt ... a lot?"

He, Bautista, answers me with scornful movements of his lips: "Only later, when I stopped in the woods, above that weird village. I felt a sharp pain in my lungs ... and I think my heart started skipping beats—for a moment."

The things that Bautista talked about! I asked him about his scar! No doubt it hurt him, so what was up with that "only later" business? And it must've spurted blood, too, for a long while, Bautista's blood … dark, aromatic … but—why does he talk that way … about the woods his heart his lungs? Maybe they stomped on him, beat him … boots on his lungs … so yes, that's that. Actually it is!

All of a sudden, for no obvious reason, Bautista asked what my name was. Strange! He must've known it from before! What is even more odd: my hand rested regally on his shoulder (this detail wasn't provided for in the script; it was spontaneous and unfathomable); love, on account of sudden intimacy like this, emerges as equally possible and impossible. A few minutes. So indeterminate: hope and betrayal in the bodies and movements (not the thoughts) of Jelena Belovuk and Bautista van Šoven; it's all totally straightforward, run-of-the-mill, on a broken-down park-bench (the backrest) at the end of the park! Bautista was an unmoving monument; a statue from an unknown sculptor. (No shocker here: unknown people always deal in famous ones.) An unwound and rewrapped Egyptian mummy, on a bench, in the middle of the Balkans, but from Chile (the internationalness that is archeology); I tell him that. He laughs and wants to kiss me.

"Have you heard of the last name Belovuk, and my first name, the given name Jelena?"

"Of course I've heard of it!"

He then abandoned the idea of a kiss. That man! That Bautista, the man who looks like Bautista, the Chilean, and anyway he said it so tranquilly. I told him, with my legs asleep up to my belt, that I was Jelena, the Belovuk, a flutist, and I also told him:

" … You know, I play at parties, special events, promotional gigs, commemorations, and sometimes I do piano actually (I'm so conceited) and there are the regular old meetings, not always, though, regular old meetings of associations of scouts, hunters, mountain climbers, kite enthusiasts, and the like."

And Bautista, bewildered:

"What do you mean by promotional gigs … and is there music at a commemoration?!?"

I told him briefly about how group members promoted themselves for president, vice-president, treasurer, corresponding secretary, recording secretary, etc., especially the ones who were the best in that discipline. But he was even more clueless after my explanation, and he asked:

"What kind of … what did you say … associations … What are they?"

I whispered to him, bringing my lips (they were moist in the corners, and I know that Bautista saw this and wouldn't be able to resist it) close to him: "People who use various things have banded together, and enthusiasts, exhibitionists, adventurers, in fact everybody, absolutely everybody, you know the ones who love to get undressed, feel each other up, kiss, and pinch one another in grottos and caves, and mountaineers, you understand mountaineers … in a shared association, you know, in this country everybody, and I mean everybody, partners up, and music and merry-making at commemorations, well, that's the new regulation thing here, d'you see?"

"And Jorge and Ricardo played the flute"—one couldn't tell which one of the two of us said that. But then I said, more softly than just before:

"Do we wanna ... hey, Bautista?"

Bautista didn't wait; he didn't think twice (and after all, all of South America was flowing through his thin veins); his hand grabbed my right breast convulsively, powerfully, as if it were a banner of Chilean liberty. He clenched and tugged, pulled in the direction in which Ricardo and Jorge had run, a long time ago. Then my breast flashed between us, for a ragged part of a second, and I didn't doubt my eyes.

I felt a quiver, piercing like a needle or a thorn (semi-passion), in actuality an asymmetry, for Bautista was pressing the tip of one of my breasts. The experience would have been completely satisfying if Bautista had taken hold with the same force, the same grip (positioning of his hand) on my other breast too, and in the same spot—a fruitful political alliance. Two Chilean hands, dark-skinned, for my two little fires, at their peaks, right on the edge of the nipples (it's like we were in the Andes); would Jorge and Ricardo have also been this unsymmetrical, if they had been sitting ... across from me? I pressed my fingers to Bautista's scar, and just for an instant he grimaced in major pain (this political alliance is indestructible); gruffly, convinced of his power and superiority (an alliance between two member states always works to the disadvantage of at least one of them), Bautista spoke:

"Your nipple is so tiny that it fits comfortably into the gaps between my teeth, and even more comfortably in the gaps where I have no teeth; so spacious! This is unfortunate. Women in Chile have nipples big enough to plug up the mouth of any scumbag for good."

We stood up from the bench absurdly stuck to one another (in the eyes of other countries not party to the agreement, an alliance is always a ridiculous tie, and a bit sad, too), wet and smiling; once again I pressed on his scar (the spoils of the stronger country) and said:

"Bautista, the women of Chile have taken on a really big job then."

CHAPTER SEVEN

Propellers, Motors II

I flat-out dragged Aunt Maša into the borough offices in Palilula. She'd gotten angry and she wanted a suitable husband for me and not Vladica, a photographer with hairs growing out of his nose. She made no effort whatsoever to understand our marriage arrangement, a tie which was, at any rate, a friendly one, and which we were making official on account of Vladica's student loans. On the other hand, though, Maša understood perfectly well a few other things: my loneliness since Marijana's departure.

At this strange ceremony, the veins in her neck and on her temples bulged with anger.

When the registrar in Palilula, Anđelija, asked Maša the witness whether I was such and such a person, Jelena Belovuk in the meager flesh, she wrinkled her brow and answered in a near-scream:

"That's her ... Jelena Belovuk ... but I don't know who that bum is!"

Anđelija thought that we were all in cahoots (including Aunt Maša) in some illegal activity. I screeched with laughter. Aunt Maša beat a demonstrative retreat from the bride-and-groom registry office. The man who we had on the street a few minutes before the divine comedy asked to be a witness, promising to buy him drinks at the *Žagubica* until closing time, in extreme perplexity approached Anđelija saying that he was 1000% certain of the truthfulness of our personages and the accuracy of our names. Anđelija then did the deed as fast as possible (she read us some marriage regulations in legalese, asked for our assent and about changes to our last names) and without congratulating us left the room calling out the roll of the next grooms and brides ....

Those were the words used there (on the marriage license). And there were other words (right by the staircase, above the public spittoon): don't spit on the floor, and then two arrows with awkwardly printed letters: divorce room and marriage room.

Vladica and I got drunk at the *Žagubica* that evening with the witness. Our *kum*, the witness, a chance participant in an equally chancy undertaking, had no doubt done good work: at the last second he had convinced Anđelija, talked her out of thinking something illegal was going on. After the *Žagubica* closed, we gave our best man-witness some money "as a loan," wished each other "every happiness," "good health," and to boot he wished us "two children at a minimum" and we wished him "an open tavern close by" and we headed out in opposite directions. My now personal photographer Vladica and I walked arm in arm one foot in front of the other down Grobljanska Street, on foot to Milaševa and the thirteenth floor (the elevators had been out of commission for a week). In the tiny kitchen by the balcony there wasn't a crumb to be found, not a trace of any kind of food, nor a swallow of any type of drink except for the water that dripped persistently out of the busted faucet. Vladica said: "Above all we need to replace that rubber washer," and then he took some paper (a few sheets from a composition notebook) and wrote down one after the other:

To do in marriage (Now), things great and small, Now or Never:

1) submit the application for my loan
2) describe in detail our material circumstances mention with a sentimental smile that Jelena has only Aunt Maša the retiree and I have only Jelena
3) obtain confirmation from the university (grade-point average) convince Stana this one time just between us of course to raise my GPA
4) get that loan it is mandatory that I get the loan
5) buy a new camera—if possible a Nikon sell Jelena's television for it Jelena's dresser Jelena's necklace and all of Jelena's other unnecessary items
6) take a trip with Jelena as soon as possible to Dubrovnik
7) in Dubrovnik sit next to that Orhan Restaurant and those very photogenic boulders, lounge around in the shade and remember them
8) buy at the first opportunity 30 bottles of Coca-Cola for me and for Jelena that purple wine in Montenegro, on our way back from Dubrovnik
9) after Dubrovnik and our fun at the Orhan prepare to take half of my exams half will be enough

10) immediately this very minute make an extra key to Jelena's apartment

We didn't talk. I read this scorecard over Vladica's shoulder. Then we cut off the light and lay down; I on my bed and my photographer, my personal one, on Marijana's (former) bed in fact the one that was hers till yesterday; they were dusty, as old as the hills, and the torn woolen mattresses were stacked in layers on the floor, one over top of the other: these beds, Marijana's and mine.

Vladica and I were good friends, especially after that horoscope, the belching, and the incident at the airport. And that's precisely why I asked him why we couldn't sleep together, with collegial motives. I told him that was the best way to become definitive, sworn friends and to stop being shy around each other when we changed clothes, got undressed, picked our teeth, went to the toilet, burped, broke wind—had all those momentary uglinesses, swollen faces in the morning, and similar things. Vladica showed not the least sign of surprise; he did, however, start to sniffle and giggle.

"OK fine, Vladica, but I'm not quite that unattractive!" I said to him.

"Jelena you have freckles on your face, small breasts that no man alive could settle for or settle down on yet you have this megalomaniacal need. All right, so your skin is beautiful. I saw it. Nevertheless, your hands are rough, like a manual laborer's, they're cracked, and they're larger than mine. Your legs, hm, they're pretty long ... For me as a photographer the most important thing is that you unwittingly manage to remember to

50

coordinate the color of your eyes and your blouse, those freckles the shoes and your buttons—always yellowish-brown. Photographic harmony. Other than that … when you sit … like tonight I mean … when you were sitting down at the Zagubica, your knees were gleaming white, and you know that excited me a bit, in the moment, like an electrical impulse up my legs, across my stomach, but … now, in the dark like this, if you mean now, in a nightgown with cold cream on your face, well, no dice. I can't get into it! Downstairs the streetcars are rattling past, that lunatic neighbor of yours is swearing away, Bosa your confidante is wheezing from the strain of sex and smoking, and that ancient wobbly bed of hers is shaking, d'you hear?

I can't do it … collectively like this, with all of Milaševa Street or when even two floors, the 12th and 13th, in a Milaševa building …!

And incidentally, we're just friends ….

I remembered … hey, Jelena, you aren't asleep. I know what to do: let's line the walls with styrofoam, whadda you say?"

"Vladica, we can't … The apartment is rented," I tell him, and he, convinced that it would be easy, practicable, and consequence-free, said:

"It won't hurt anything, styrofoam—and if we put it up with a little glue it won't leave any marks and we can always take it all down …"

"Okay, Vladica, we'll settle this tomorrow. Good night."

I thought with bitterness about how my personal photographer Vladica, my good friend, didn't understand anything about friendship. With my eyes open in the darkness, with the streetcars and Bosa underneath me, I thought to myself about the bad start to this day and about a couple of other things having to do with styrofoam.

In the morning, Vladica got an ample breakfast, an ironed shirt, clean shoes, and money, and off he went to hand in the neatly filled-out application for a loan at the student credit union. Thus the first point on Vladica's marital scorecard was neither geographically (formally) far from Milaševa Street (the loan office was on Nemanjina) nor distant in substance, for he would, certainly, get that loan.

And the other items on the scorecard (which amounted to a crumpled pile of little pieces of paper ripped nervously out of my music pad, staffs and all) got crossed off at lightning speed (fulfilled) by Vladica's Parker pen.

After a month he had even acted on item five—he'd bought a Nikon, sold my dresser, tv, transistor radio, some books, my necklace, and all my albums, "unnecessary since you don't have a record player," he said.

Somehow or other, when our friendly marriage had gone halfway (as pertains to the [in]famous agenda items), and by that I mean as far as the Orhan and Dubrovnik, the wine and the Coke, Vladica crossed out beginning with the sixth point (dealing with our joint excursion to Dubrovnik and our mutual enjoyment of wine, or rather Coca-Cola, and our shared seats and tables alongside the Orhan right at the flank of a photogenic boulder) each and every one of them and instead of all that he'd written in one single new point:

Propellers, Motors II

Travel to Afghanistan or Iran (Tehran) or Nepal or all of the above. How? Sell the Nikon, Jelena's fur coat, my typewriter, my optical slide duplicator, projector. Travel by train and hitchhiking and bus. Without Jelena.

I got a few pairs of socks and underwear ready for him, undershirts, and one pair of pants; he was wearing a sweater and jacket. These few items (he didn't take a single book, or his old camera) I packed in my water-proof red backpack along with my sleeping bag, which had been doing double duty as my quilt. I saw my personal photographer off at the train station, and kept him company till the train to Istanbul arrived. Somehow he pushed his way into the throng of people standing on other people's feet or on one foot, their own. He promised to write as soon as he had a chance and update me on his address.

This was in December. I believe that Aunt Maša's birthday was on the same day that Vladica left. I don't know which birthday it was.

During all those days that didn't come to pass in this internal arrangement, I had grown, completely, and it seemed to me irrevocably, bored with myself and with Bosa. Aunt Maša was all I had left, as a possible source of strength but only once she had calmed down. And even when she had calmed down, my forgetting her birthday would provide a new occasion for sulking. Regardless of the fact that the forgetting took place at a time of intense anger, something that for Maša did not constitute an extenuating circumstance. What should I do in the meantime? From fury to fury? From the conservatory to that sometime Bosa? Or from Bosa to the potential (one day to come) Marijana, if she were ever to return; if I take her; to Vladica's letter, if ever he sends me anything at all?!! What do I do in the meantime, in anticipation of all these events, in expectation of the time that will be incomparably shorter than the meantime! What do I do then, now (eternity is at stake) if no one is concerned with me.

I started with stupid things: I put Vladica's first and last name on the door (took mine off), then I bought a ring for 20,000 dinars (on the black market); I kept in mind the wise advice of my friendly husband to the effect that with wedding rings, white on yellow, one should skimp, you shouldn't buy them, or you should buy only the ones that run you a minimal sum, by no means, however, should one cut corners on flute cases (they wear out and people change them a lot) or on photographic equipment. Vladica claimed that no one notices if it's real gold or not, and no one will notice if I'm wearing a real fur or not. His second piece of advice, which simply proceeds from the first, was: one should at every (realized) occasion deceive people, all people, without exception, nor can friends be spared this; it's a maxim, a general principle, an imperative, which naturally admits of no, as if there could be by force of law, exceptions and therefore it must be strictly and inexorably upheld.

That piece of advice (legislative principle) I began (in my own interpretation) to apply at that time, in the days of the meantime.

The little grocery store, two streets down to the left from the entrance to my building, is where I did almost all my shopping except for bread. I started going there frequently (four times a day), trying to get the grocer, who was not a bad-looking guy, to notice the yellowish wedding ring. I pushed it under his nose (when paying I kept my hand on the cash register or next to it). I don't know if he noticed it, that grocer, my ring, or not, 'coz he just kept saying to me:

"Whatcha need, missy?" or "What'll it be today, girlie?" or "Does the little lady need cigarettes for daddy and the neighbor again today?"

Really, he was pretty good-looking, and that was despite the fact that he reeked of vinegar, ammonia, sweat, garlic, heavy-duty *rakija*, all mixed together. Although his presence befouled the entire grocery store, and even after the next worker showed up for his or her shift, bad odors didn't readily clear out of the store. I turned up regularly (with frantic persistence) exactly four times during his hours and shopped especially passionately for silly little things, all sorts of stuff, whatever.

I was pondering how, when the stinky grocery boy (yes, that can draw attention) goes back into the storeroom (which was next door there on the main floor) to get sugar or flour, I assumed he would remain there for a minute or two since I had asked for five kilograms of one thing or the other; he had to pour it out of the large sacks and therefore maybe he would need more than a minute or two, and especially if I were to ask for five kilos of both flour and sugar. More time would be necessary for him to do that, and I would make use of that time, I would go after him, close the door, and push the grocer over onto the flour or the sugar (no matter which) and crawl his frame like 55 kg of flesh and bone.

That's what I was thinking, I didn't know what I really wanted, but in that grocery store the buttons on my dressing gown came undone of their own accord. He, the stinky grocery boy, always said, taunting:

"Button yourself back up, neighbor, this is a workplace ... and you're not my cup of tea ... what the hell do I care ... there's the shop and the customers ... but if I felt like it I'd close up this place in a heartbeat ..."

He was arranging some colored ribbons when he put on a stern face and repeated:

"For God's sake button yourself back up there, neighbor! They might come by to check, and then I'd get punished on your account, plus it would be unpleasant if a customer showed up ..."

Ashamed, I buttoned my clothes back up, constantly justifying myself to myself the whole time:

"I have to take in these damn buttonholes ... I didn't think anything of it, but you know how these slots get looser."

So I did my shopping in the store of that grocer who made such a fool out of me: razor blades, after-shave, condoms, hard liquor ... all of it just to spite him. And he (the cad) would stand there smirking and stinking as he asked: "Guests ... more guests ... hmm little neighbor ... not bad at all ..."

But there weren't any visitors. If only there had been anyone at all! Like the pedant I am I stacked the groceries I'd purchased in a cardboard box. I wanted to send to Vladica, as soon as he notified me of his address in Afghanistan or wherever he might be, the things he needed!

Bosa began keeping to herself. She had a man and he locked her door as if it were his own. I couldn't get into her place. I felt really sorry for the strudel, the innumerable pieces of it that disappeared into that guy's belly. That guy of hers. And just how good some of Bosa's strudel would be, and her lousy *rakija* after an unsuccessful rendition of the *spiritoso* movement (Concerto No. 1 in G major).

Most of all I wanted though a man who would have enough strength to drive his shoe in between the frame and the door, his big ol' shoe, and shove the door, the door to apartment 128 (with his divine-masculine strength) with a bang until it hit the opposite door jamb, even though I was bracing it at the time with my entire body (55 kilos of flesh and blood versus the power of a real man incarnated in his mega-shoes) propped against the radiator.

But none of that happened. I was waiting for Vladica to send his address, for Aunt Maša to get a grip, to blow her top again and then get another grip, and then, for inconsiderate Marijana to appear again inconsiderately in a dream or in the doorway, or in some other reality (it exists), and I throw her out, and bring her back in, everything about her's tied up with the word: again; or that I unbutton the grocer's fly and demonstrate in that manner how he has overcome his fear of inspectors and his shame in front of customers. The meantime is a blank. I go regularly to the music academy, to my lessons, to that unhappy Pergolesi, in fact he is only unhappy in my hands, on my lips, on my flute; it took so long for me to be able to play the whole *spiritoso* through to the end, without going back over any of it. Professor Radić, of course, never stops believing that I am irredeemably lazy, that I don't practice at home, but I do work hard at it, he knows that, and I play my flute everywhere practically non-stop. Truly, I lug it everywhere with me, onto the streetcar, into busses, grocery stores, and concerts. I return to Milaševa Street, apartment 128, with the flute in my arms (Maša says, "My simple-minded Jelena, instead of a child she rocks a flute in her arms") and bags of groceries. Some down-and-out types intercept me (not always), in the entranceway, and then I run up all thirteen flights of stairs and pound on the door of her apartment (out of fear) and Bosa's man screams out:

"*Schizooo!*"

The meantime rounds itself out, and the chances are slim that some small spot somewhere would split open, making a hole for time and other things to start leaking in, and then get inside and distort it, and turn its viscera inside out, letting the air dry out the mucus of the meantime. That's the situation. A condition but not a process, where nobody, just exactly nobody, is interested in me, not even from a distance.

In the morning, every morning, all seven of the neighbors on my floor and I exit our apartments at the same time (7 am). I'm the quickest; I run as far as the elevator, insert my key in the lock, place the hand with the ring, sort of rest it, on my bundle of keys and on the lock, on the top part of the lock. I don't remove it till the elevator arrives.

The neighbors have read the names on my door, and seen the ring, listened every morning as I call out before

I lock the door: "Bye, Vladica ... I'll be back at the usual time," and "I'm blowing you a kiss!"

So while we wait for the elevator (with them looking at my ring-bearing hand-dove) they ask affably, indulgently, every morning:

"How's your husband ... Is he recovering?"

In a very serious voice (I force myself to think about funerals, messages of condolence and other sad things so that laughter doesn't make me burst, like a balloon does from getting squeezed too much/too hard on one end by its string) I reply every morning:

"He's ok, but he needs bedrest for another few months ... You know, those vertebrae heal very slowly ... " They nod in understanding and counterfeit emotion and say simultaneously, "What can you do, neighbor ... *C'est la vie*. You just never know from one day to the next what life gives or takes away, but he is young; it will pass. He'll be better soon. We just want to see him alive and happy, yes." Sometimes, however, they say "happy and healthy" or "alive and well" or for example they might say "your husband" one time and "our neighbor" the next, and so forth. Every morning the same Eucharist with the neighbors; and shortly after that, the removal of a glove (it's January) at the bus stop (so that my wedding ring is also in evidence there). In the evenings, upon my return, that man at Bosa's place yells, curses at me, and calls me a schizo, and hot-to-trot and a big fat bitch.

At the beginning of February, however, something changed. The meantime had given up. For example: I buy men's shirts, size 41, and carry them unpackaged and unfolded over my arm, home. After that, Maša was well along on the way to recognizing me again as her niece, Vladica sent photos (where's that camera from?). Marijana isn't to be found anywhere. Bosa's off on a trip to Igalo.

For the neighbors, I continue to put up with a spoiled, admittedly sick, but good-natured living husband.

CHAPTER EIGHT

Aunt Maša's House Rules

A unt Maša has no one but me since her husband, Anton Pavlović, passed away.

Anton died suddenly; unexpectedly, for Aunt Maša, and unprepared, for Aunt Maša. In recent years he had devoted himself to sports and to love (with Maša). He went to all the basketball games and soccer matches. Maša used to tell him that he took exaggerated care (indirectly) of his muscles, stomach, hair, heart, complexion. "Indirect," my aunt Maša would say, because the late Anton took so much pleasure in sporting events of all kinds that it was as if he were participating in them himself. He'd return from the games as exhausted and moist as if he'd been working out. Maša formulated it so clumsily, illogically actually, because Anton's athletic exertions weren't a care of his but rather heedlessness. Perhaps Maša's interpretation, however, was not totally off-base. She would tell Anton that he was way past his prime, the peak of his vital powers, and that he shouldn't expend pointless energy trying to get those years back and that there was no need to build his muscles up psychophysically as if he were 40 and not at least

60 years old. "At your age, baskets, excitement, whistles, nets—your heart's going to explode, Anton; it can't stand up to changes in the standings, exclusions from the Champions League, the European ... or like the world championship ... missed goals, 'chances' ... 'chances,' oh Anton, your heart's going to blow to pieces ... Please, Anton!"

Maša was truly worried whenever she caught sight of Anton, flushed and sweaty and foaming at the mouth on account of "blown chances," she tried to discourage his zeal for sports and the bursting of his heart, from that definitive "basket" so crucial for Anton, for the two balls, duplicates.

On Saturdays Anton bought for Aunt Maša (she explained to me in detail) chocolate bonbons with a single ulterior motive: for the two of them to kiss across the candies (in their mouths). Maša understood that to be concern, or a way to maintain passion, potency.

Then one Saturday, with bags of chocolate bonbons in his hands, Anton simply tumbled to the sidewalk, a few meters from their apartment on Tsar Uroš Street. It was a few minutes before the time he typically began the Saturday ritual of cuddling with Maša. That's the way he just up and died, with a sweet thought on his mind (via the candies made of chocolate).

Aunt Maša sold off all their furniture after the funeral; she got rid of his things, of everything that could in those trying days remind her of him. Anton had existed, but now he was nowhere to be found, and she needed to start thinking as if he had never been there or anywhere. In that spirit Maša began automatically cutting off the tv whenever games came on. "Ball" was a word that you couldn't even mention around her. At the children who wished longingly for a ball in the stores, or played with one, or simply toted one in a net or an Adidas bag, Maša stared at them horrified. She sounded deranged and kept saying: "God, make these whippersnappers see, and realize that they are carrying around their own heart unprotected, in plain view, unwrapped, dirty, muddy in an Adidas bag, in a mesh net, or under their arms, pressing down on it with untrimmed, dirty nails. Make them hide it from view, wash it, wrap it, and preserve it!"

I moved into her place. Maša's rehabilitation began with her tutorial organization of my life in her house. She specified strict time slots for my showers, sleep, meals, practice, dates, doing my make-up, chores, and other things. The only part she couldn't control was my time at the Academy.

She thought stubbornly about my marriage, not about her own. On the bathroom door, opposite the mirrors (wise auntly strategy: she hung up her house rules with a heading that was both emotional and ridiculous: "From Maša, thoughtfully, to Jelena." She had framed it, the way people frame house rules and such on trains, in hospitals, and schools. Under the title stood, literally, the following:

a) Sleep 8-10 hours. Sleep leaves your face harmonious and fair. Men don't like bags under the eyes, paleness, yellowness, grayness-malaise, you know, in your face. And they also don't like the morning

crude in the corners of your eyes, even if they are
blue like yours.

b) Don't use gaudy make-up. It's not natural.

c) Don't remove hair from your legs but you can
from your underarms!

d) Wear a girdle or hold in your stomach! Your
stomach is always distended.

e) Stuff cotton in your bra (at least for the time being). You have the breasts of a thirteen-year old
girl. Mine were bigger than that at age eleven. But
you're over twenty. You've missed your chance.

f) Wear smaller shoes!

g) Let your hair down—always over your ears, so
people don't notice right away that they are asymmetrical—wash it regularly, dye it blonde, you'll
remind other people of me when I was young.

h) Wear high heels. Others will think you're at least
as tall as me.

That was the first part of the Innkeeper's Laws. It
was printed in neat letters. Below that last counsel-
imperative, underneath the letter "h," Maša had written
sloppily and awkwardly (I'm certain of it) "I wish you
happiness greater and more consequential than sports."
She had pressed a kiss onto it, leaving a smeared red impression.

After she had pointedly processed the issue of my external womanliness like that, and resorting to a few
tricks of the trade, which do have their historical foun-
dations (the feet of a geisha, cotton in the bra—and a
strictly controlled lust for food that blazes up and is

canceled by established anatomical dimensions—corset-smooth flat stomach): nature in hair, in a sweaty face, blushing, and in bright eyes (myth blended with history—megalomania in a woman), nature according to a recipe; the recipe emerged at breakneck speed like a basketball from the omnipotent experience of Aunt Maša, and techniques (reducing one's foot size from a 40 to a 36) as a method of regulating nature; Maša switched to motherliness. That was treated in the Rulebook: "From Maša ... to Jelena": in only two places, that is, in two points:

- a) Jelena have as few abortions as possible—at least before you have a child, after that, do as you wish.
- b) Jelena—do yoga. For a smooth and painless delivery; the babies will fly out of your stomach like rifle rounds and crash down among people like wild animals!

That divine Aunt Maša of mine! She has planned out descendants for herself, and some descendants they are! My child the bullet. One unique shot. A beast.

The third section consisted of a treatment of my internal womanliness:

- a) Jelena you are not required to become the world's best flutist.
- b) Don't take such paint to show (prove) your braininess everywhere and at all times!
- c) Be indulgent (gentle and broad-minded) towards men and their largely sensitive dispositions, at least at first!

Maša's infamous proclamation was but an attempt, along with other attempts (not recorded) to make a woman out of me. Even if it was just by enlarging my breasts with cotton; or covering with my hair long and blonde my asymmetrical, "freakish" as she would say, ears. "At least for the time being." —that came up several times in Maša's proclamation. I didn't have a clear understanding of Maša's "time being" or "at first," or that possible, unspoken "other" or "second" time. I never asked her if she in her female life put these two ideas into effect: "first time" and "second" time. Where did she, tall in her youth, beautiful, big (she used to say that the tailor's tape measure fit snugly around her), feel better, in the actual time being, or in the second, potential time, or does she cherish the time being like someone else's baby cupped in her left hand and the other time hangs unsteadily from the thumb of the same hand?

My Maša got all worked up over false eyelashes, or the ponytail allowing so impudently for the tragic asymmetry of my ears to be discovered, and in addition she got angry at me for not even trying to wear shoes any smaller than size 40s. I did not fulfill the items she connected with her motherhood. I think she struck closest to true with those. Aunt Maša had not had any children, not even any aborted ones. She wanted grandchildren, of course; she'd tried it all, from yoga to buying self-help books, the old kind and more modern ones and the latest expanded editions, and then the book: Your Child and You. To no avail. Finally moved on to practical approaches: she stood on her head, with her feet twisted and her palms turned up behind her, and she would change positions, and rest in a pose (position): "the tree," and she'd sweat and go red in the face in an attempt to focus her thought (from inside) that is to say her eyes on an unmoving point. The years made of her body an irregularly shaped mass, swollen and soft. Her inflexible legs, together with her large belly, resisted every movement that required stretching. She gave up.

I came to the conclusion that Maša's concern for the realization of descendants, for their genesis, had to be great when she allowed the capillaries on her face to burst from her extreme exertions during yoga that she was doing with the intent of encouraging me and goading me on.

This seemed to me like: Maša had been defeated; she was holding no further methods in reserve. Strategy turned into direct aggression; she ceased giving me money, she restricted my cigarettes, prepared only vegetarian food (on the pretext that it was healthy); not a single time did she buy wine. She was angry in the most earnest of ways. There's no doubt that Maša was adept—even when she was beyond the bounds of her preconceived tactical plan; she scored hits on my most sensitive and needy zones. And yet once again nothing happened. Not because I'm an especially decisive and unwavering person, but rather because I never succeeded in finding the means by which I could placate her.

Two years of our life together passed, and not quite three years since Anton's death. Some changes in the notorious House Rules: "From Maša ... to Jelena": did occur. She stopped thinking about my marriage. And she started thinking about her own—but her thoughts about my children continued. That hare-brained Maša wanted me to give birth to a child for her and then hand it over to her like some precious relic, for future rule books and organizations on Tsar Uros Street.

I began working with an orchestra. Conservatory was finished. There was a man (he showed up), about Maša's age. He didn't make me a single baby. He didn't have enough strength in him for a "bullet-beast." I ran myself ragged (it's true) for a third year, as did Maša's dachshund, who mated with my leg, the heel of my shoe, and my arm. I stayed quiet to the exact same degree as the parrot, Otto von Bismarck. Wise animals—dogs, parrots, and I, Jelena the dolphin, more and more absent-minded (with dirty hair and grubby dirty nails), well-intentioned like a dolphin and vindictive. Aunt Maša exactly like other aunts sensed this and didn't reproach me with anything anymore. Sometimes she'd quarrel with the bristly-haired and petulant Otto, and she would bop the dachshund on the side of his head—that is how all occasional bursts of anger seep into the wise and forgetful heads of animals. She had made peace with my small breasts, big stomach, infertile husband, and greasy hair. Just sometimes, over breakfast, which had long since ceased being vegetarian, she would ask:

"Jelena … When will there be …?"

"Be what, Maša?"

"Oh you know … "

"You mean … a wedding, Maša?"

"No … I don't mean a wedding, Jelena."

"Then are you thinking of ... grandchildren? Is that it?"

"Well ... yes."

"I don't know, Maša ... Be patient a bit longer. Maša, I can't, just like that ... !"

Then I would kiss her on her cheeks with their powder and rouge and she would always ask, timidly and always incompletely:

"Why ... that ... of yours ...?"

"What is it, Maša ... Say it."

"Oh nothing ... nothing."

It was always like that. The half-conversation always ran like that, along with Maša's vacillation. What she meant to ask was why "that guy" didn't divorce her, why he didn't leave his wife, I know that's what she wanted to ask, but she never asked it. After a good-natured and confused "Oh nothing ... nothing," Maša would get angry, start to rage, and say that I, I of all people, was going to kill her, her heart like Anton's was going to make its "basket," "goal," that it was going to split and race right into the net—under the ground—in a narrow, marked-out area. She mentioned grandchildren and her weak and worn-out heart and always in the same manner: she'd clutch her chest (somewhere around the heart), asking me in a panic for her Ansilan ... water ... and Ansilan again; then she'd demand I make her a coffee, "her final cup of coffee before she goes to meet Anton," and with a slow step she approaches her animals. She whispers something quietly to Otto and starts to tickle her dachshund around his long ears, life rushed back into Maša's "paralyzed" body after the coffee was consumed and then Maša's perpetually "weak" heart would await the next opportunity. Maša with her eyes open wide in astonishment would say: "Jelena … a missed chance … that was only a little bit short of being the last goal."

CHAPTER NINE

The Secretary of the Tenants' Council, and a Volunteer

After Marijana's flight, and after my pointless and ludicrous marriage to Vladica, the photographer, but before of course it was before the passing of my uncle Anton Pavlović, I rented a studio apartment in a newly finished building, I don't want to tell you what street it was, or the building number and floor. Not because I don't want visitors—I haven't lived in that flat for ages—but so that you won't create any difficulties for the secretary of the tenants' council, a man who would not be able to defend himself!

It was like this: as soon as I had carried my belongings inside and turned the lock on my door, two times around, somebody rang the bell, just once, and gave a solitary tug on the door handle. I opened up; I opened the door wide; I always open up doors all the way, yep, without any reservations, and: the man who rang, and about whom I want to talk to you now, he was already seated on one of my suitcases, and on the other lay some of his papers: what speed; fantastic!

"But … who are you? What do you want? Why are you … " I pose these questions to him as I am closing the door, perplexed.

"Oh, I forgot to introduce myself, bustle bustle, don't take it amiss," and he stood up, came over and kissed my hand, "Secretary of the Tenants' Council, as a volunteer, retired department store manager Martino-vić … Petar Martinović.

"I don't want anything to drink, I'll thank you in advance … nor coffee, just here to work on my list, you know child, we have to keep track of things … *yeees*, we have to keep track!"

"Yes, of course, you … you have to keep track of things … but what's the issue here … I don't understand … so you … and …."

"I'm all booked, sold out: I'm supposed to go around to 125 apartments and that, my dear young lady, comes to 600 persons, did you know that amounts to 600 persons?

"What kind of … persons? Military ones?"

"Well, *reeenters*, miss, *reeenters*. Six hundred persons."

"Big building."

"If you only knew, miss, what kinds of people are out there, 600 persons … and there are probably murderers here, too … and there's even this one very famous Belgrade prostitute living among us, God only knows exactly where she has this apartment by us, and I mean, really, miss, who'd she get it from? Yeah: who could have assigned an apartment to her yes, my dear young lady, there really are all kinds of people out there; and this is not to mention the cholera … oh, dear … cholera is knocking at our door, and there really are all kinds of people out there, but me, I just keep the lists!"

"Are you thinking of smallpox?"

"Those're the same thing, darling … Isn't that right, aren't they the exact same?"

"But who … I'm sorry … who cleans this building? You know, I just got moved in, you can see for yourself, and I don't know where the bins are located, the garbage cans, and I mean, where's the custodian?"

"Have you seen—heck yes, you've seen, if I may say miss there's no building to be found anywhere that's this clean, if you eat off it, pardon my language but it wouldn't even make your tongue dirty if you licked it, damn straight you have seen those large pictures downstairs on the ground floor, is that right you have seen them … well I will tell you, nobody can help but notice them."

"Uh … what pictures?"

"Well, downstairs, miss … How can you not have … big like frescoes in the entranceway to the building, flowers, red, blue, ah, in all colors!"

"So that means … the construction company, I mean whoever built the building, that means they put up those pictures, and are they photographs?"

"Oh no, missy, don't you understand that when I say pictures, it's clearly like frescoes … downstairs on the facade, you just go on down there for a jif if you want to have a look at them, they are very beautiful, I can wait for you down there, I mean, I've got that much time, d'you want to?"

"Fine, fine … I'll do it later … So do you know, who, those, the pictures, I mean … who … painted them?"

"Ah, there you have one of the beautiful things about this building, my dear young lady, down there on the ground floor lives an especially fine gentleman, an invalid since the war; he can't sleep you know not the whole blessed night and it's then that he beautifies our building."

"What's up with that ... with him not sleeping?"

"Well, miss, in his body he has a total of twenty bullets, with some of them even in his head and at night it's like these bullets turn into vampires. They prowl in the dark, you know, and will not give him any peace; it's sad, sad, young lady."

"What did you say about the garbage bins. Excuse me but where are they located?"

"Oh geez, miss, if you knew the kind of cleaning lady we got (the secretary of the Tenants' Council nodded his head and used his hands to show what kind of cleaning lady it was) a woman like this, five kilos of chocolate we gave ... yes yes ... a bit to these folks, a bit to those folks, and it had nuts, sweetheart, with hazelnuts, all five kilograms included hazelnuts. We stole her. Now she's ours, and she's like this (demonstrates afresh with his hands), child, she's tremendous ... .there's no one like her in this whole entire district of the city."

"How's that ... chocolate? How'd you ... steal ... a woman ... I don't understand?!"

"But it's phenomenal ... child ... I tell you what; with pieces of sandpaper, child, she cleans, I mean who does that anymore, only cabinet-makers, little one, only carpenters!"

"What ... only carpenters ... .what do they have to do ... ???"

"All right, little one, come on and let's get you signed up … I don't have time to gab … c'mon missy."

"OK, but … go ahead … what kind of registration do we have to do?"

"Girl, listen now, I have this little dingbat, er, I mean a daughter, and she would dance on this table right here and now, would she ever, you know (demonstrates with his hands) that Gypsy music … She or me we'd jump around, or she'd invite me to join in or me her … to dance, sweetie, the two of us oh yeah …."

"Gypsy music?"

"Yes, girlie, you know, all animated, the blood just boils in your veins. You know. Right?"

In my bag I had a bottle of vodka that I had just purchased; since I had not bought any glasses, however, and since I didn't already own any that were packed, I gave him the bottle. So he could just have a drink with no further ado and he drank; and … I did, too.

"You know, miss, my dear, I can see that you are well-meaning and sort of lonely, you're lonely isn't that right, but you know, I would never do this kind of work for money, I'm a volunteer, where else have you seen that, come on, be honest: nowadays who's a volunteer for anything and what's more for the Tenants' Council, and 600 *peeersons*, miss, that's not a very small number; I've got a nice little pension, it's not big but it's just enough for me and that … my … daughter, you know … and they tried to get me at KOMGRAP, the construction company here, yes, yes as an accountant … I almost agreed … but I'm supposed to make a trip to Australia, you see … "

"Australia?"

Yes. You know the routine: to visit my nearest and dearest ... Qantas-Jumbo-Superluxury—Giant streaks across the skies and you're full steam ahead and lickety-split there you are with your loved ones and your pockets full of money ... in an hour's time ... in no time at all ... yes, indeed, young lady ...."

"So who ... do you know ... over in ... Australia?"

"My brother, my brother ... not by birth though ... my cousin ... but he is my brother ... Well, he lives there ... In Melbourne ... miss."

"In Melbourne! Huh, that's interesting ... but isn't that a long way to go?"

"Goodness, missy, you apparently don't read the newspapers: with a jumbo jet nothing is far off, and also you drink for free, and you can eat ... and watch the stewardesses, you can watch for free, and even films, music, ah, that's Qantas for you ... say miss, what do you think, should I also bring over my ... the ... dingbat?"

"Dingbat?"

"I mean, my daughter, child, didn't I say I have a daughter! I don't know. I don't know; I'll have to think about it. By golly but she could cause a scandal ... You understand dear! She could start dancing, bouncing, and Lord knows what all else, you know what a scandal is ... I'm an upstanding man, so ... It'd leak out, get around, and see I have never, ever done anything ... nothing at all ... nada, you know ... I mean the rumors and the gossip and such but I never you know and me being seventy already ... there's never been anything at all ... miss ... no type of cheekiness, no inappropriateness of any sort ...

76

and especially not with women ... never, ever, everything's on the up and up ain't that right missy I know you were brought up well, I see that, I respect that ... oh but that chickadee of mine ... well it's awful; but all right, miss, let's do this registration ... so these are my papers here, I'm responsible for them ... but ... I won't have anything to drink ... Gave up coffee ages ago ... "

"Okay. Go right ahead. What is it that we need to register?"

"Let's get started once and for all, miss. My fountain pen here is drying out ... as you see I'm holding it open; name!"

"Name? Ah. Jelena."

"Last name. For god's sake, miss!"

"Belovuk."

"Belovuković! I had a friend; his family name was Belovuković ... but he's dead; he died last year; hey maybe child he was some relative of yours? I'll put down Belovuković. Yep."

"Belovuk ... You know I'm Belovuk and not Belovuković!"

"Well, all right, missy ... It comes out to the same, the exact same thing ... at one time it was without the '-ić' and now it has the '-ić.' You see, young lady, nothing has changed because it changed when they were one and the same I mean the exact same people isn't that right, miss? For crying out loud, I know a thing or two too, and before the war I was a dance instructor ... yep ... young lady ... and after the war ... Belovuković was there, yep, and I was teaching dance ... that's how it was miss just so you know!"

"Dance? As in dance floor?"

"Oh yes, child, that's right, on the ballroom dance floor, you betcha; Viennese waltz, tango the Argentinian one, the foxtrot that's still modern today young lady, *yeees* … they all come to me, ones like you … young people … girls … It's still in demand."

From my bag I took out a small tape player; on the tongue of the secretary of the tenants' council (while he spoke, his tongue was visible) I spotted a large wart; simply unbelievable, I know, but he spoke completely clearly and intelligibly despite that growth; what a moment for "heavenly music"!

"My goodness, miss, but that is beautiful music … isn't it, though? Whadda you know? … Goodness, girl, my little dork would certainly love this, to … Shall I call her, missy? Do you have a sec?"

"Did you know that this is Herbie Mann, the flutist … Do you listen to music for the flute?"

"Oh … I know, girl, I know this, it's like what Boki Milošević plays!"

"But that's not the flute."

"Whadda you mean it's not, eh, come on now … I think I'd know … I was a ballroom dance teacher before the war, child … I know what a flute is … but like how—I watch him on television—does he ever twist around while he plays … that's what I find very interesting, child, and spirited you know, like Gypsy music … oh yes, now, that is the flute, yes, I know, dear, what that instrument looks like."

"No … that's not a flute; it's a clarinet. Look, I'm going to play something on this, a composition for clarinet,

just so you can see how different it is from the flute …
You know, I—"

"Don't go teaching me things, child; there's no need.
I'm 200% sure of my musical education … an instructor
on the dance floor for so many years … that's no joke,
miss … so many years … my dingbat knows it, too …
What's a flute and what's a clarinet, oh, come on now!
Let's finish our work!"

"But … hold on … "

"Listen, girl, I don't have time I'm all booked up, hey,
I need to look in on 120 apartments, and then some … I
have to collect the contributions … I'm the treasurer
even, volunteer basis … but somebody's got to do it,
and who would it be if not me right? How many family
members that is members of the household are there in
this apartment?"

"Huh? How many family members?"

"On account of the water, child, but I guess you
know that much … How many members means how
much you pay … D'you understand … and I have to
take down your line of work, *yeees*, dearie, has to be
done!"

"I am … just me … I rented the apartment, you
know … I live alone, and well, you can see … I haven't
even moved in yet … and you're already here … You
see … This is odd … strange. I think your organization—that's just fine!"

"That means 1 family member. I'll write in a '1' but I
seem to think three or four, right, child?"

"But it's only me … here … Only I will be living
here."

"Oh *reeeally* now … and yet that's not how it will be; first addition, your boyfriend … c'mon now, missy, don't say you ain't got one … a beauty like you! And then, then there's his sister or brother, no matter, that's your second additional unit and that means two members besides you therefore three miss and then that girlfriend of yours who only comes by sometimes isn't that so missy … I mean I know you young people … I have a chickadee down there … that … daughter of mine … I know how it is … and water has to be paid for and I'm writing in … the young lady's the one but I have a foursome in mind … just stored away … you for future reference … a big leak or when the faucets drip … nobody but you can pay for that … eh darling?"

"But, I mean really, didn't I tell you that it's just me here … "

"*Occupaaation?*"

"Student … I'm studying at the … "

"Student then. That means the law school, eh, young lady?"

"No … I, like, study at the … "

"Aha … I know. I know, missy, what you study … You study foreign languages, ain't that right, well, yes, *languaaages* and by the way you're pretty enough to be a model … I guessed it; did you, dear young lady, know that I have perfect intuition … everything in advance … yes, everything, every itsy-bitsy thing … even my … daughter … could confirm that … I know precisely what someone has been up to; and so you see, just now I guessed at one glance that you study foreign languages, tell me it ain't so … What do you say?"

"So listen ... you are wrong ... I don't study foreign languages and if you really want to know I'm at the—"

"All right. It's not important. I'm writing here, girl: student, and the rest: what how where, etc., isn't important but I still do believe I guessed it right!"

"You didn't guess it right and you can't guess it but as you say it's unimportant, isn't it? Incidentally why would the tenants' council need to know how I spend my time, how is that the business of anybody in this building?"

"Come come now, turn down that Milošević a little, and please ... Now I'll write out your receipt for the contribution, it's voluntary ... but everyone gives ... just so you know, everyone gives ...

"How much is this ... contribution?"

"Just 10,000 dinars, missy, and you'll admit that isn't a lot ... and all kinds of things might need to be repaired, right? Eh?"

"I ... you now ... don't have ... not now ... to give you but I'll have it tomorrow or ... the next day ... and then, I can give it to you then!"

"All right, dearie ... It is voluntary ... but everyone gives. Just so you know that everyone gives, then I'll come tomorrow good-bye, miss, good-bye ... Have a nice day, dear ..."

The next day, Petar Martinović, secretary of the tenants' council, as a volunteer, showed up at 7 in the morning; he rang the bell, pounded, and tugged on the door handle until I opened up.

"Oh geez, miss, you mean you're still asleep and it's 7 o'clock already ... But did you get your hands on that voluntary 10,000 dinars … *noooope*! But miss I don't have time to keep coming by every hour … But all right, not important—next time—mmm … child you haven't had … your coffee … Oh, I knew you hadn't … Intuition, my perfect intuition … And to think that my little dork made some … Now I'll just … I'll bring some straightaway while you just go get dressed and wash up.

He returned swiftly with an ibrik and little cups on a tray, with the inevitable log-book under his arm and also with his chickadee, that is to say, his daughter.

"Here's some coffee … and here's my daughter, I was telling … There you go, get to know one another … Can we sit on the bed; I see you don't have chairs … You could have brought some, Ljubica … Next time … next time we'll bring some when we come! And now you wouldn't want to play that flutist Milošević again my Ljubica would love to hear it … and can she show you how she can dance so whadda you say?"

"You mean the Herbie Mann?"

"Well now, my dear young lady, I mean Boki Milošević, he's that excellent flutist, I was telling my Ljubica …."

The next day they came by yet again, only this time with chairs, and with coffee again; we listened to Milosevic the flutist, a.k.a. Herbie Mann; as if it were important in the least what his name was! It's all the same, exactly the same, as Petar Martinović says—flute or clarinet, Herbie or Boki? It doesn't matter because it's very much the same.

That's how I came to socialize with Petar Martinović, and his dingbat Ljubica, her name was Ljubica, for a whole month, that's how long I lived there, in that fully painted building. But I didn't give them any voluntary 10,000 dinars; at first I didn't have it, and then when I did have it, I didn't see them, and later would spend it … and in the end I forgot about it and also Petar Martinović, the secretary of the tenants' council and in addition a volunteer, stopped asking me for it, certainly he forgot too after what happened, so, huh, what happened oh about that … about that I don't wish to tell you anything, just so you know though there was something!

Much later, after Jelena had recounted all of this to me, I read in the newspaper that Petar Martinović, retiree, had died at a pedestrian crossing in his 72nd year of life. And I heard some rumors about how a hospital had asked for his body, that is, for some of the organs so they could be transplanted, because it had been, supposedly, verified that at least half of them were in extraordinarily good condition, especially the heart and the liver; they had the required permission, the signature of one of the members of the Martinović family; some woman turned up who was unrelated to him; it turned out he had no family, and she demanded money, a fairly large sum of it, mostly for his heart.

CHAPTER TEN

Playing Chess on Dositelj Street

Ten o'clock at night, in the 26 bus:

The only two people, aside from the driver and the conductor, are the two of us: I, the first flutist of the city, Jelena Jelenska, as sweet Mića would have it, whiter than Greenland white; to which I would add: the whitest person in Belgrade; he, the man, a man of indeterminate age, was standing at the far end of the bus, looked to be tall, looked attractive. What more can I say about myself in the moment when the 26 bus goes past the monument to Vuk, and one part of Roosevelt Street is lit up, at that instant I felt not a whit of nostalgia for that apartment on Milaševa, and what could I say other than that I am no one's! The bus stops, moves on, no one's gotten in, I am barely staying on my feet (upright), bouncing around, and I'm holding on to the upper bar tightly with one hand, in the other is my annoying and unavoidable flute. Do I feel a sense of belonging there on bus #26, with which I travel every day from its point of origin to its terminus for no reason, and I like it, I especially like it, when

I can lean my flute against someone's back, no one's flute against nobody's back. I keep up an extremely intimate connection to bus 26, but I do not belong to it; I am no one's field, seldom worked, with rye or barley, thistle, and stinging nettles … and some unknown thorns (they aren't blackberries), my clothes don't conceal it; but why the flute? I have no idea why … there's not even anything about it in my dreams; I don't get called to join public concerts, they say I don't practice enough, that I don't show up to rehearsals on time, and I'm liable to be late even when there's a concert; it's their mistake; and the part about the flute every day being nestled up against my pelvic (it is a bit swollen from such) bone, and on strangers' backs, that is, on nobody's back on the 26 bus, and in other places, that's an unmusical fact, they say. Only occasionally I perform something, stand in for somebody and also just now and then give private concerts to people out there who have no connection to music, such as the cats in the courtyard and stray dogs. They tend to listen attentively to me and not ask any questions, and as alley cats and roaming dogs do, they yawn afterwards.

The man, who, like me, is getting jostled around—the driver's going too fast—he's holding a creased newspaper, a pile of newspapers, and a big bag with something printed on it: *Buy all your pretty things in Belgrade's department store.* We're turned in such a way that we are facing one another; I'm interested in whether he saw the streetlight at the corner where Roosevelt Street starts, and all the insects there! Our glances intersect on a center line that's invisible, and curved a little; it passes through the small

slit on the middle doors. It's Friday; he, the man of indeterminate age, is going home after work! No … He isn't
heading home from his job … He has no briefcase;
where's his briefcase? He bought something; he was on a
shopping run … Maybe … for clothes … in a department store, that bag is big?! Or maybe he's carrying his
clothes from the dry cleaner's?! Wait, no; at the cleaner's
they would've given him, you know, a bag … theirs, with
a different logo, an advertisement, like for instance *Get all
your clothes cleaned at the Terazije drycleaners—we guarantee a
total clean.* I know! Actually he's moving. But of course,
why didn't I get that earlier! That's his bag, he kept it
from some earlier purchase, he's moving, that's obvious;
surely he is transporting, on the bus like this, a few ran-
dom small items that could fit in a bag, perhaps socks and
his shaving stuff.

He's watching me; I'm reading the letters above his
head: It is prohibited to pester the driver; he looks at my
chin, my neck; does he see the red lines, horizontal lac-
erations, from rope, as if they were from rope? My green
shirt is unbuttoned; I read the warning again, and then I
lower my eyes a few centimeters, but he is of middling
height, and my gaze gets thrusted into his minute eyes,
his piggish eyes, like on a piggy.

What am I supposed to ask him if we meet up in the
middle doors? Surely I'm supposed to say something to
him. I can't slide by him just like that!

We've passed the Theater: last stop, the brakes grate,
a swerving, the opening of the doors.

I got off through the rear door, next to where I was
standing. He exited through the door up front; it was

87

closer for him. We walked towards each other, but it still seemed like we intended to cross the street in different places and would then proceed in reversed directions. As he drew closer I thought: to me he does not look like the type of guy who keeps used shopping bags with department store logos on them, and ads for cigarettes, clothes, perfume—that he had bought two years ago, for example, in Paris, Trieste, or on Terazije, at the "Beograd." No, he's certainly not one of those; he's wearing a threadbare gray coat ... but perhaps he does keep nylon shopping bags among other things?

He approached; he almost touched me ... he, the man, in a gray coat with a bag in his hand; he wants to tell me something, his intention is to communicate something to me, and wouldn't you know it we didn't meet at the middle doors of the 26 bus! I see a very splotchy face, wrinkles and a dimple on his chin, simpatico, and I smile!

"Do you find something particularly funny?"

"I do ... But why do you care?"

"Well ... I was thinking you see ... We rode together from the first stop to the last stop maybe you ... have noticed something ... that I didn't! So ... we just spent at least half an hour in transit in an ... empty ... it was empty ... bus, and that ..."

"So what if it was empty?"

"You know, I thought, it seemed like ... well, before you gave me that smile ... "

"I didn't smile!"

"It seemed to me, before that ... that I knew you ... although I would not dare bet on it, you understand, there's no way I'd swear to it ... no way. I never gamble, that's not by the way my way of doing things and, taking risks, there exist, you know, better ones. There exist better risks, chances—do you see what I mean?"

"But in regard to this wouldn't you want, wouldn't you dare to wager it's true?"

"Well, you see ... I told you, I wouldn't dream of betting ... and it ... you understand ... that I knew you ... you know, when you smiled just now, suddenly it was a different face and not the one that I thought it was, and that's odd, those two faces, get it ... "

"I don't get it!"

" ... the one face that's different, and then when I saw you, you remember, in the telephone booth, surely you remember, the one at the Café Grad, oh but you must recall it, you know the one without any glass, no glass divider in between, on one side, you know ... in the other booth, next door, there I was, with you in the first one, and then so I think I turned to you, I had said something to you ... "

"But ... I don't know you and ... I don't know, I don't remember this ... in a telephone booth. I don't get it."

"Whadda you mean, it's quite possible. I think it was very much you, you really don't remember but these are the kinds of things people do remember. I spoke to you through the glass, through that opening where the glass had been, said that you reminded me of my friend, my old schoolmate Jelena, and you said that you weren't that Jelena who was my friend from school."

"Well, as you can see, I don't know you."

"Wait! … Don't go! … I mean I've met you so many times in the 26 bus, and at the concerts … at the Kolarac, where I go regularly to hear you … and on two occasions, I believe but I wouldn't bet on it, I sat next to you when you weren't playing … and too we live close by each other … You know, my place isn't far from yours, two streets over, three blocks, three little blocks, and the streets are little too, we are so to speak next-door neighbors … "

"But I do not know you, I do not remember you, and I don't know your name … and what do you want anyway? For crying out loud, what's wrong with you?"

"Hold on, please. Here, I'll tell you my name, look … so you'll know … I'm not some thug, or a con man, if that's what you're thinking."

"Well, all right … Knock yourself out!"

"I live on Dositej Street, right there, right there in the first block, by the Theater, you know that little bar also called the Theater … yep, right there … Ristić Ristić Vladimir, I live alone and have absolutely not the first relative in Belgrade, my people you know are from a village not too far from Smederovo and … I don't even have friends, that is I mean to say that the people I hang out with are likely not my friends and that we don't pal around in that way, but rather in another way, almost certainly not, though again I wouldn't bet on it, who knows, maybe they are my friends, and it's that way just to spite me!"

While we were having this conversation we had already moved quite a distance from the bus stop, and it seemed to me, but I wouldn't dare bet on it, that we were halfway to my house. We had just walked past the emergency clinic on Simina, when Vladimir Ristić suddenly halted, saying it'd be best if we went up to his place; he said it was "here right around the corner, second door, second floor." He also said that there was certainly something to drink there!

Naturally I went around the corner and through the second entrance and up to the second floor, like with an old acquaintance, whom I'd met again in the 26 bus after such a long time.

Truth be told, Vladimir Ristić was an acquaintance of mine; he did know me; I couldn't say how he just turned up like that, materializing through the walls of No. 26, when I know that he too boarded, nice and simple, and often, at the first stop and he exited at the last one, and now, I really can't do anything about his being my acquaintance; and one time I actually had seen him at a concert but it wasn't at Kolarac; Ristić was lying about the Kolarac part, lying like a rug; there was nothing to it … I didn't hold it against him, it was trivial, the Kolarac thing!

He cut on the light; I was hit by the odor of sweat and dirty socks, grease and headcheese, bologna and stale air; immediately I saw pictures on the walls they were cut out of newspapers and framed in dark wood some of the frames even had glass and they were all small-format, like postcards. One of the photos was of a guy with a beard, a bulging forehead, and a narrow mouth; way down at the bottom was a signature; of course I was astonished when I also saw a newspaper photograph of Jean-Pierre Rampal! What connection did

Vladimir Ristić have to flutes, and how was it that he had even heard of Rampal! On the third newspaper photo was a child!

I asked Vladimir Ristić who the man with the beard was and the bulging forehead, and what the child's picture on the wall is supposed to mean, and how it was the he had heard of Rampal! I didn't ask that.)

He tells me that "the guy with the beard" is a deceased relative, a well-known Smederevan, and he adds: "You've certainly heard of him!" I shake my head at that, at his relative, the late well-known big cheese from Smederevo! He reached this conclusion derisively, Vladimir Ristić, and it's no wonder, for, as you can see, he says we Belgraders usually don't know, in fact we know but we forget, but usually we just don't know the names of famous people in small cities, so says the kinsman of the famous Smederevan; and staring at me he asks where I've lived, where I was born, whether I also have some celebrated ancestor, if my parents are noteworthy citizens. He's thinking, probably, of whether they are politicians or something like that. I reply that he also, probably, has never heard of the renowned hospital, upon a major hill that is also renowned, where an even more renowned me was born. I tell him, celebrated even in the hour of my birth, on account of the alignment of the stars, and because of the irreplaceable sign of Aquarius, and I laugh unrestrainedly. He, Vladimir, is persistent, investigates further but isn't interested in the facts but rather in these pauses between sentences that he would use to mention again his relative, late of Smederevo, and express doubt that I really hadn't ever heard of him. He says he was a national leader, one of the heroes of his day, in that region, a music pedagogue! I laugh even harder and tell him, insolently, that he is laughable and that his relative, Mr. Deceased Musical Pedagogue, a tribune of his day, of the people, is ludicrous, too! Suddenly Vladimir Ristić puts on a serious face, points to the photograph of the child and says that this little girl, a relation of his, was a genuine mini-Mozart. But she died and didn't make it to big Mozart status. I shrieked with laughter and said I didn't believe him not even the littlest bit, and I told him his dead little relative, the great musical hope, the little Mozart who wasn't able to grow up, was ridiculous too; I asked him if perhaps he was related to Rampal too, the greatest flutist in the world, he must be some kind of relation at least on his mama's side and why wouldn't he be? Vladimir Ristić said that it was nasty of me to laugh and poke fun that way, when he was telling me the truth, and that his little relative had made it into the newspapers because she had died from getting the wrong medical treatment. He didn't know what she had been suffering from, but he said he put her newspaper picture up on the wall because he liked her face, he had no other photo, the same way he liked Jean-Pierre Rampal's face, although he had never listened to him, and until he saw this photograph and the caption under it, he had not even heard of him; he said he couldn't understand at all why I was mocking him so hideously; he actually used that word: hideously!

And later, after our conversation about his musical family, I got embarrassed!

"Do you … do you perhaps have a chess set. Do you play …?" I had to think up something in those moments of silence and waiting as the water came to a boil on the hotplate there in the little unlighted hallway, but … I didn't know what I would … It was a drag, all of a sudden it was a drag … and then I didn't want to go, but maybe I did, I don't know now which it was! But that's why I know for certain that it mattered to me that this man not think I was dumb or cowardly. I've never tried to explain myself to myself, however after the incident with Vladimir Ristić, who had on the walls of his room a genuine little musical encyclopedia, it occurred to me, like a bolt of lightning, the way things are revealed to lunatics, the crystal magnificent thought, something like a solution, a global solution to global issues, like a condensed science, all at once, to them, to nut-jobs … so also to me, the idea that everyone who would ever get to know me, would be obligated to think of me, to speak of me as about an exceptional person, with amazement, not with pity at all!

"Yes, I have a chess set … and you would like to play with me, ok, fine; but it's not going to go well for you, but all right, fine, if you insist, if you have the irresistible urge, *theeen* I've nothing against it, nothing at all … Just so that you know there's no taking moves back, no 'oh I forgot,' no slip-ups or re-dos, no wrong moves because 'I couldn't see it, the lighting is bad,' etc."

He took the chess set out of his armoire and I saw that it had been underneath a heap of crumpled sheets. He cleared off the table with one motion of his arm, some papers, cut-out pieces of colored construction paper with graphs drawn in thin lines of red and blue, they landed on the ground; they scattered around the table and covered the floor. Then Vladimir, with his head pressed against the horizontal edge of the table, began blowing with the intent, probably, of blowing away flakes of ash, bits of used eraser, and dried little flies pressed almost flat. He still, however, had to do the cleaning by the most efficient method of all: he wiped the table with his hand (palm) and then wiped his hand on the leg of his pants, then the table again, and the hand on his other trouser leg; as soon as he finished, he placed the board on the table. Then he went to make our coffee; he returned from the gloomy corridor with an ibrik, cups, and some ancient napolitanke cookies on a tray that said Greetings from Vrnjačka Banja.

And then:

He switched off the bulb in the overhead light and turned on a small nickel-plated work lamp. "Conservation of electricity," he joked, as he pulled up his trousers while (he makes a small crease above his knees) preparing to sit down, halts in a singularly attractive position; I feel his firm taut limbs much closer, as if he had shifted a little, then he dropped into the easy chair. Boop. Just like that, sprawling legs with carefully hiked-up pants, above his knees, so they wouldn't drag on the ground.

"Concentration of light," I say; and I throw in a secret thought: a magical triangle; out loud I say: "Like in the Atlantic, not far from the islands of Bermuda."

"Yes ... yes ... but what did you say, just then?"

Vladimir's first move, c4. I inform him of the fact that I know no theory, but that I am helped in everything, I mean in chess, by my intuition, and I saw also that I can sometimes pull off a whole combination right down to the final move, but that I am not conscious of doing it, for as I tell him in my head in the center for sight black and white get mixed up, and I imagine that my own figures are the opponents'; for a moment, and I tell him that he, I know it, is certainly a better player.

He moved his knight to c3. He had to lift his hand, for I was completely bent over the table, to touch my hair, inadvertently, and then to make his 3rd move. My response, of course it was totally injudicious, thanks to that airy touch. He laughed. He lit a cigarette and smoked it, peculiarly somehow, from the side, as if he was going to break it; and he looked at me, and at the board, and he laughed again and looked to be think-ing … This got on my nerves; why procrastinate; we had only just begun. I tell him there's no reason to have to think so long. "There is," Vladimir replies. "From the beginning on. It is imperative that one de-velop an operative, factual, and psychological strategy." I tell him I don't understand although I know that it's part of a psychological strategy to look alternatingly from my face to the board. He warns me, with no rea-son at all at every one of my moves, to watch what I'm doing because you can't take anything back as a result of pretend oversight!

"Do you like saffron?"

I don't say anything.

"Do you like saffron? … Huh. Do you even know what saffron is, what it looks like, who uses it and why, tell me do you know?"

"I know … and anyway … "

"You want an ashtray! Feel free to knock your ashes into the ibrik … but of course it's no matter, don't hesitate … so why are you uncomfortable here? … I do not understand you at all I do not!"

The game was advancing. And saffron was the reason that Vladimir was able to force my mistakes, saffron and that touching!

Steam is coming out of my nose I'm so angry, and I stub out my cigarette on the table. He laughs; the table is polished, and now there's a little mark there; and he goes on smiling.

"Didn't I tell you that you wouldn't be able to … just … with me … "

"Hold on. Wait … "

"I told you there's no taking back moves. Why didn't you look? And anyway you still have a chance, come on now, why aren't you playing? Do you Jelena believe that killer whales are the smartest animals? You know it's really interesting, that evolution thing, something's gotten a bit confused here, aha nice rook to f8, a good move for you, and by God things don't seem to be the clearest with that evolution stuff, I mean evolutionary theory and there you can see how it is that the most intelligent are the killer whales and not the monkeys, let's say … "

"Well fine, Jelena, do you want to play I guess you haven't stopped … and don't, I urge you, your position is quite good, it's not fantastic and neither is it all that tragic, but watch out, don't do that prematurely … I mean don't you see that the pawn is weak … "

He's watching me, staring at me non-stop, I am such a feeble opponent for him, that he doesn't need to look at the board while I move!

"Don't you want to give up? Right, good chess players always give up when they determine that the situation is hopeless, aha, you're saying that you're not yet convinced, you're not saying it but that's what you're thinking, isn't that what you're thinking?"

… … … … … … … … … … … … … … … … …

I said nothing the whole time that he was babbling … He never stopped talking!

… … … … … … … … … … … … … … … … …

"All right, all right, don't get angry. I'm not suggesting you do any particular thing, but it is nonetheless … but it would be better for you to concede, it's objectively so and I would concede in your place … It will be less painful for you … But about your giving up, it'll be checkmate on the next … Fine, fine, I'm not saying anything … but would you like me to turn on the radio, just tell me if you like music, you know on Fridays they play all night … and hey you never told me do you like saffron!?"

He talked and talked like a wound-up toy: "You can't concentrate, but why! That's stupid of me, my talking disturbs you. But I was thinking it would be easier for you to relax if there's some background noise that's why I wanted to switch on the radio … Just imagine what it would be like, the deathly silence in this room, and with me not talking … We're strangers, however, and you know you don't know me at all; it's true that I have seen you around, but I don't know you, it's, like, by accident that I know your name … and then … You came here, it's different than if I had gone to your place, you understand … .?! No, wait, don't leave now, wait … Hold it! … ! I mean … we have to finish our match! Wait wait please! I didn't mean anything bad by this what is it you think I do for a living, didn't I tell you, I'm a technical drawer, I did tell you but you forgot! Fine! Sorry I did not mean to offend you. See, I'm sorry, forgive me, so, if you want to … Relax a little , so we can finish … You can lie down, I'll just move these papers … and then you can go wherever you want, it's cool, it's cool, I didn't say anything, make up your own mind … "

"Oh go to hell … What do you want. I'm not at the psychiatrist's office; relaxation, you say … bullshit … and that … that stuff about knowing each other and not knowing each other … I don't want to finish our game, I'm leaving this instant, I'm going, I must go … No, no you didn't offend me but I have to go, it's already late, past midnight, and I really do have to go … "

"Do you want another coffee?"

I had gotten to my feet and I don't know why I sat down again, I do not know to this day why I stayed there in that apartment, on Dositej Street! I can only guess that it had something to do with the idea that all people have to think well of me and how can't be allowed to pity me in any way.

"Voila, the coffee has arrived": he slurps as he drinks it, and he drinks it hot; "Maybe you'll be able to pull out a draw, but you'll have to pay attention, or maybe a tie … You're improving. Damn, you are getting better, hm, yes, umm, we can see thaaat!"

"You … you … you are a big f--"

"Excuse me, what are you saying, I mean no, Jelena, sorry, but I am not a fraud … that's what you meant to say!"

"No … I didn't mean to say that … but you understand … that psychological strategy of yours, well it's obvious that you launched a little ship made of paper, that waterproof kind, for instance, and then (in the bathtub, of course) with your hand you make waves, stir the water into motion, and the little boat rocks, danger at sea, it should abandon its voyage, but you're persistent, you push it out into the middle and for a moment you stop making waves, everything is in your power, isn't it; then you make another storm, the little boat tips over, it looks like it's going to sink, but hell no there you are again, you let the water (in the bathtub; all of this is happening in the tub; therefore the space is clearly bounded, like those bearded and beardless figures of yours on the walls) settle down again, you allow the imaginary (of course) captain of the little boat to think that he just became the luckiest fellow in the world and then he turns to face it again (naive galoot), turns his face back around, whipped until just a moment before by the winds and then, without wasting a moment (you abuse the trust of the captain), you create a flood, this time the little ship really is almost on the bottom, but once more you are there and so on, from the top … "

"I understand that … but … why do you call yourself a 'little boat,' I mean you, Jelena, you're a real yacht, fancy and luxurious, wait … Hold it I'm not as dumb as I look. I know that you were not thinking of yourself, but rather of your chess position of my strategy … but what do you want, I guess you mean to say that I urged you on, and deceived you, and that you didn't have ti--"

"You, you, you are an idiot, a common skunk, a dope, and of course you are just as stupid as you look … 'deceived' … Now you're going to say that you seduced me, you (at this moment I stood up from the table, clenched my fists in the rush of a colossal rage like a volcano, not from a bathtub, and therefore not demarcated, but rather completely without borders, like a volcano that inundated those graphs with the red and blue lines and the common commonly astonished face of Vladimir Ristić), what were you thinking with that … 'yacht' … you said 'yacht,' you hick, bully, you fake … " I had grabbed my flute and my jacket from its hanger in the foyer, opened the door, and screamed villainously: "Idiiiot!" I hadn't managed to take the first step when he took me by the shoulder, pulled me inside, and slammed the door. He was shocked, and I believe baffled at being thwarted!

"Let me go! For God's sake … leave me … get your dirty stinking hands off of me, you redneck, you vulgarian!"

"Quiet, quiet, they can hear everything … Why are you screaming, what's wrong with you! What has come over you all of a sudden, for God's sake, Jelena … so what did I do to you what's wrong with you, calm down! Why are you trembling … " (Vladimir Ristić is shaking me; he shakes out of me, like I'm a bag, something out of that bag, that man does this.)

"Do you want some water … well okay then … I'll see you home, it's late, you can't go alone … Not if you're this worked up, do you want an aspirin, you have a headache!"

… … … … … … … … … … … … … … … … …

"It doesn't hurt? So why are you rubbing your temples?"

"I'm not rubbing anything; it just seems like that to you!"

"You are rubbing, how could you not be rubbing, now are you going to say that you didn't scream, when you woke up the entire floor, definitely, they're going to think I'm some kind of maniac … They'll start avoiding eye contact … It's better nevertheless if you take aspirin when your head is hurting a lot!"

"But I'm telling you I don't have a headache!"

"But why won't you, I mean, take it! Here you go … and some water, and what's wrong with you … It's not poison … You'll feel better, you'll see, and I'll walk you home when you've calmed down a bit!"

"Come here … into the bedroom, you can't hang out there in the dark like that! Feel free to come in … You can also lie down for a bit, I won't touch you, there's nothing for you to be afraid of … and you did wake up the neighborhood (he laughs) … come on it, take that aspirin already, you say your head doesn't hurt … as you wish … I would … just to help you … I see that you are overwrought!"

… … … … … … … … … … … … … … … … …

Several hours after all of that:

He, that man, seriously thought that I had gone crazy, and he hastened all the more cunningly, and of course more swiftly, to make use of this license that my mindless being so lavishly offered him. He smoothed my hair and said something, mumbled half-asleep something about smooth skin, about lies, about false eyelashes about futilities, about cunning phenomena that are here to hold us back, about women, all of it vague and unclear!

And my face, he didn't touch my face! How many times had he touched the Smederevan's bulging forehead alone, how many more times had it been touched than he had lived, if he existed, how many more times than the number of years turtles live in the Indian Ocean, which have exactly that kind of back, convex and prominent.

CHAPTER ELEVEN

The Lookout

(The Words of the Anonymous Man Who Longs
to Love Jelena's Body)

I first saw Jelena, the red-haired flutist, on the street; she was shining white, like the moon, and she expanded and swelled gradually, as she walked; that whiteness of hers was teeming, the way bread swarms with yeast. Her skirt did not cover her knees. The red-headed flutist tottered on high heels, to the left and to the right, a female Colossus, as unstable as the tower in Pisa.

Take me at my word: I fell in love, scout's honor, with Jelena's body, not all too firm.

At a meeting of the recently founded association of hunters, scouts, mountaineers, ditchdiggers, kite-fliers, paratroop scouts, and all others who, as volunteers and amateurs, climb, descend, fly, sail, or hunt in nature, under it, above it, whether from cupidity or pure enjoyment, it was there that I saw Jelena, blue and red and white, for the second time.

She was sitting three rows up ahead of me, twisted to the side (at the time I thought, with tenderness and a touch protectively: from scoliosis, spondylosis, and every other kind of rheumatic fever, epilepsy, and inhibition I will, conscientiously, cure you, Jelo … Jelena). The curls of her hair were intermeshed with the back of the chair—her hair was that long, immoderately so— and she smoked, also immoderately.

When Borisenko Ristić, the president of the association, came in, slamming the door with a bang, she, with a cigarette clamped between her teeth like a street punk (I'd break her of all such crude behaviors) detoured around pretty much the entire hall, and sat down two seats to my left; and otherwise both of those seats would've been free. I consider that to be an unambiguous sign, just as unmistakable as when you raise your whole arm, stretching it out from deep in your shoulder joint, so you can wave to someone pulling away from you on an express train—a sign that she likes me. Well, I mean, it's clear the flutist circled around the whole room and sat down two seats away from me on the left, although the hall (and especially that row in which I was seated) was full of empty spots. It's clear why she did that. She made no bones about feasting her eyes on my physique. Exhibit number one: I am the biggest and most handsome man in the hall. Considering the fact that the row was half-vacant, the illusion was created in me that everything happening in the hall was actually occurring as a prelude to the symbolic union of her body and mine. And so the following things happened:

Borisenko Ristić, the world-class mountain climber, pulled a checked handkerchief out of the inside pocket of his suit coat; with brisk movements, left and right, he wiped off just half of his neck, clearing his throat, and in a quiet voice he said a few words, none of which were intelligible. I believe that those words were directed at the enchanting Jelena, or that they were uttered in reference to her, for Borisenko Ristić, mechanically and evenly rubbing his neck with the handkerchief, stared shamelessly at Jelena with his one eye. As he did so, his second hand tugged at the ends of the bandage that covered his nonexistent right eye; the bandage was firmly fixed on a diagonal from above his right ear, across his forehead and above his left ear, and ended up in a knot on the back of his head, that is to say, near the nape of his neck. The story is that some brute of a man intercepted Borisenko Ristić in front of the door of his building (not far from this very spot) who, mentioning something about revenge, a cliff, a mountain pass, dug out his right eye with an ordinary kitchen knife. Later on, people whispered that Borisenko Ristić, an alpinist with a global reputation, was covering up someone's death in the Alps, for example, but whatever—maybe it was atop some other mountain somewhere else. In addition, it was whispered that on the night that that cold-blooded avenger stabbed him in the eye, Ristić broke out all the panes in the entrance door to the building, and, screaming, kicking over the flower pots with flowers and the flower pots with dried-out dirt in them in the walkway, raced frantically through the building for a long while, till just before dawn. The custodian, Milka, and her two daughters, unmarried girls (with no immediate prospects for a happy re-homing), all three were present at the meeting at which they mourned equally for Ristic's eye, the broken glass, and the overturned flowers; about their ficuses, aloes, cacti, and who knows what all other flowers, the housekeeper was to speak for days with visible sorrow, as if she'd lost someone of her own, a husband, for instance; the malicious women in the neighboring apartments immediately circulated stories that Milka the custodian and her two nubile daughters grieved more over their plants than they had previously over their husband and father, respectively. Since that unpleasant incident Borisenko Ristić, our esteemed president, had developed a cough and frequently, very frequently (I've had occasion to make sure of this) checks his eyepatch, and takes it off and puts it back on.

Now he moved aside, his hand was shaking, his body also, and with no shame whatsoever he removed the bandage, revealing a huge hole, a swollen red eyelid. Then I noticed that (she was watching everything, with her blue eyes) to Jelena this was not the least bit unpleasant. However, Borisenko scuttled, with uneven steps, over to sit down, catching sight of the two empty seats, between Jelena and me, grinning obscenely, while doing so, next to Jelena. His checkered handkerchief, forgotten afterwards, after the hysterico-exhaustive sponging off of his neck, remained on the secretary's table, behind which was seated Marko Štrucić, the passionate underwater angler, otherwise known as the director of the association, and the recording secretary Vjera Nikolić. She, with an expression of disgust on her face, pushed Ristić's checkered handkerchief off the table. No one bent over to pick it up; I think this made President Borisenko truly uncomfortable. Marko Štrucić leafed through file folders, pulled out a few papers, and handed them to the portly Vjera. All the while one-eyed Borisenko threw his arm over the back of Jelena's chair, touching Jelena's curls, that much I saw quite clearly. Then Jelena turned around and asked me to roll a cigarette for her; she gave me both tobacco and rolling paper, of the type "*Vážka Olšanské Papírny*." She said she enjoys more than anything smoking domestic tobacco, from a cigarette holder, but she couldn't begin to roll her own cigarettes, and furthermore it was so unpleasant always to have to bother someone for some trifle like this. That's exactly what she said: "trifle." I told her that there exists a little machine you can buy that will roll your cigarettes for you, however she waved me off and laughed and announced in a somewhat sharper tone than she sort of enjoyed watching adroit male fingers (surely they're also skillful at something else) as they, although it only lasts a few seconds, roll a cigarette. Jelena had moved dangerously close to one-eyed Borisenko, telling him with a laugh, as little flecks of her spittle landed all over his, Borisenko's, face, that she considered there to be a special kind of ritual between a man and a woman to be embodied in this, the rolling of cigarettes. After that, I asked her if she was a Czech, and I learned that she has an aunt who's employed in the *Základní závod* at Olšany, who, furthermore, isn't Czech but who has been married for twenty years to a Czech man. The aunt and the uncle-Czech send her boxes of rolling paper and other "bric-a-brac." Here Jelena again used the word "trifling." As I rolled her a cigarette (since my fingers were not adept at such work, the rolling lasted instead of six or seven seconds an entire minute or perhaps even two), I was considering the real possibility that this was hashish and not tobacco. What I knew about the external effects of hashishomania meshed completely with a variety of things about Jelena: all the teeth in her upper jaw were bad, the bags under her eyes were gray-purple-blue and took up half of her face, her fingers trembled conspicuously, and her pupils were a bit slow to respond.

After I had finally finished rolling her cigarette, Jelena thanked me, leaning over Borisenko to give me a kiss. So I said, you know, that blind man Ristić, the esteemed president (presidents are always esteemed) had planted himself between the two of us; actually he had sat down on the vacant seat next to Jelena, thank god … Why would he sit next to me, and Jelena had to really stretch to get to my cheek, and in doing so her breasts almost pressed (nestled) Borisenko, the esteemed president, into his backrest (just imagine the force: the force of artillery shells, of Jelena's tiny boobs) and her hand sought support, intentionally or not—because of the law of gravitation, I don't know—on the president's shoulder. I remember quite clearly, even though you aren't going to believe it, that President Borisenko began unexpectedly choking and coughing up something from his stomach, no, from his lungs; he had begun foaming at the mouth, turned red, and gotten darker somehow.

President Borisenko Ristić was blooming; his despotic masculinity was now like a mushroom. Irretrievably so!

It is still unclear to me if then, at that moment, when our three distinct bodies magnified in the eyes of everyone present in the hall (I saw: I always watch from the side, also). Borisenko, pinned to the chair, whispered to Jelena, as she gave me a wet kiss, one of his secret desires (which the association was not allowed to know), for the placement and disposition of our figures was such that the white-wolved flutists's ear rested, for two-thirds of a second, on, or close to, Borisenko's frothy mouth; from out of this jumbled mass of bodies, and not losing sight of the fact that I am always watching from the side, too—a habit of circumspection out of the life of a scout—only my head was separate, even when the flutist pressed her wet lips to my cheek. I think that everyone, in the hall, observed this irregular situation, in the former laundry that is; a hush descended like before Jelena's concert the week before, on Saturday, when she had played Haydn quartets. Director Marko Štrucić impatiently twisted his red-and-blue magic marker between the middle and ring fingers of his left hand; regularly, uniformly, the pen hit the table. A wondrous sound! Borisenko, Jelena, and I (with a heavy heart) looked in the direction of this pen, Štrucić's hand, the little circus acrobat who with grace and skill made her way between Comrade Štrucić's two fingers and flipped, entranced (by Štrucić's stupidity) in the air, inaudibly, this time because the director took his whole hand off the table, he was just leaning on his elbow and forearm now. He's impatient, that Mark Štrucić, and he stared in our direction, smiling, it seemed to me, conspiratorially. I thought, then, Štrucić is just a plain old informer, and he has found out everything about Jelena, Borisenko, and me by secret means.

An inarticulate performance; the protagonist, the flutist Jelena Belovuk, enchanting Jelena, a woman from out of poems, from the hall where meetings of a sporting association are held, a former laundry, a woman who is my own personal stinger and fallacy between my legs, Jelena the woman the high-voltage power line, the antenna sticking out of my ears, who still plays the best Haydn quartet in D-major, Opus 5, No. 1. The mastery of her execution: unmatched by Wanausek and Cora, who don't rise above the level of her toes much less her navel. Ever.

The antagonists were (including the chorus, which will turn up later) Štrucić, the director of the association; Borisenko, the one-eyed, the chief Jack the Ripper of our one-act, Vjera Nikolić, the pedantic, overweight, and detail-oriented secretary (supporting role), the houskeeper Milka and her two nubile daughters in the guise of a chorus, and I, a secret member of the society, a lover and user of nature, a scout or lookout by self-association, with fire on my fingers from rolling cigarettes for Jelena?!

Oh god, I would only kiss her knees, and nothing else, her knees as far up as the hem of her skirt, I would not lay a finger on the revolution on her breasts … or I would, maybe, at some other opportunity! But … everyone is using their stares … like chains or daggers, to slice and nail Jelena, Jelena the red, the blue hashish addict; but Borisenko Ristić, our esteemed president, an old mountain goat and a scumbag, he even touched her, under the chair, through the backrest, all kinds of ways. Our shameless chamois of a president, with his monkey arms.

Our one-act in the giant laundry room unfolded further in this manner: the ugly face of the note-taker Vjera, as fat as drab Mount Sinjajevina, broke out all of a sudden in a huge shit-eating grin. It was then that I exclaimed:

"Accordion! We're missing an accordion!"

Meanwhile, Štrucić stopped functioning as trainer and pimp to his little pencil-circus acrobat girl, and red with excitement (his very consequential role in the work of the association required such) he said:

"We'll bring along an accordion next time ... but now we want to ... before we work through our regular agenda and the new business ... to sing—and raise morale—that song "O Jelo, Jelo ... Jelena" like we did that time back when we were digging, with our common and united strength, that pit in Omoljica, searching for ... you will recall ... rare examples of worms ... and afterwards throwing in and burying the flowers that had been tucked behind the ears of our women ... and in the buttonholes of their white shirts ... now we are all, jointly, with our associated strength, going to sing "O Jelo, Jeleno ... " and we'll provide the accordion some other time ... and that Vivaldi will be played next time by Comrade Belovuk the musician ... we need to boost morale ... Milka is going to clarify to the membership a reason for merriment ... Aren't you, Comrade Milka ... ?"

Director Štrucić was a poppy. Red, like a poppy from the side of the dusty road between Pančevo and Omoljica. He was embarrassed because of Jelena and because of the song.

Once more I roll a cigarette for Ms. Belovukova, and I read: "*néjjemnéjší cigaretovy papiry zhotoveny z nejlepších su-*

rovin formula 'F'". Jelena Belovuk, all the same, is a Czech; and her aunt and uncle, Jelena's relatives, are Czechs; and her brother and sister, and her friends, and acquaintances, everyone who touches her cheek, or her hand, the hand of the flutist, all are Czechs. I'm not a Czech. She lied to me, laughing from the shadows like a mole. After Štrucić's summons, coughs were audible in the hall, as well as murmurs and everything else that had been suspended like breath held at the artful technique of the miracle worker. The man who'd been speaking was the association's second man, the esteemed director, Marko Štrucić, the underwater leader.

Jelena had, however, smoking, had sucked in and blown out the soul of the Creator (I don't know who that is), out of President Borisenko, my infatuation, and out of Director Štrucić, goggle-eyed with lust, patent, his own, with her own Olšany cigarettes.

Further minor occurrences defy any (my) rational interpretation. However, I did understand and participate in everything:

Jelena Belovuk, with a large broad sweeping wind-up, strode over to the secretary's table, stretching out her arms (whom did she want to embrace?), grabbing the papers in front of Vjera the rapporteur, and got right up in Štrucić's face, right in his line of vision like an ophthalmologist, until he dodged her by going left and right with his hand on his nose (imperative: protect the most salient feature on your face) and then she turned her back on Štrucić, who was suffocating with fear like an asthmatic under a feather comforter, and she winked with both eyes, abruptly ... it genuinely was with both eyes (it was at that time that I saw that was possible, such winking), and waving the papers, somehow less purposefully now, and she dropped them onto the table with what appeared to be diminished vehemence, between Vjera the secretary and Štrucić the scarlet-faced director. Giggles flooded the former laundry. Milka the housekeeper and her two marriageable girls tittered, squawked, and doubled over; and the secretary Vjera had lain down on the table, with her face, her large knockers, and her whole body right down to her waist lying across the papers and notes, crumpling them up.

Then things took an unexpected turn, and there was an epilogue to the one-act play in the former laundry: the mirth had not even died down before Belovuk's eyes returned to their unwinking locations, and with one stride she found herself next to Borisenko Ristić, our esteemed president, and me. All at once hands were raised as if people were voting; they wanted to have a "done deal." The hands were raised up to the level of the old laundry lines, and not a one of them was unsteady; nonetheless none of them were as firm as military salutes. And I contend that therein lies a difference, and it's not insignificant. In this conjunction—of insufficiently resolute hands and what crazy Jelena was going to do a moment later—was contained the fundamental value of this meeting of the association.

The flutist returned once more to the secretary's table, grabbed the papers and with a motion involving her entire arm (from its root in her shoulder)—as if she were throwing a discus—waved them around; then they flew all over the hall—resolutions, proposals, travel expenses, outlays for the acquisition of mountaineering equipment, and other stuff; Jelena ripped the curtain, the shroud of smoke—decisively.

She owned her wrath; with an axe she bashed in the air that had congealed between us; I felt her lips on mine.

I saw it all clearly; it was as if I were watching from the old laundry cords, from behind colorful checkered winter sheets, shirts, socks, and flannel longjohns—concealed amongst holes, the gaps in quilts, amidst the smells of starch and soap, hung on the line with my head pointed down, I also saw things that would pretty much elude the ordinary eye, a blue one, Jelena's eye. My eye, however, was colorless (then).

Borisenko was just uttering this: "I think … " when like a bullet from my hiding place (a nonexistent duvet cover) Jelena's spit struck him between the eyes, solid … and copious. And then, with quiet steps, Jelena once more as if instantaneously … disappeared. Our one-eyed, esteemed president lit straight out after her as he wiped his face with his palm; then fat Vjera, the note-taker, also ran out of the room and in the end so did several others. The housekeeper Milka with her two eligible daughters was aghast and pathetic and kept crying out:

"The horror … the horror!" and then:

"The jackass … barbarian … phooey … "

And they wanted to spit, too, at her (the unconscious need for Jelena the beguiling to be imitated in everything, including in spitting).

In the hall (laundry) Jelena's olive-green coat was left behind, tossed carelessly over the back of a chair.

I saw all of this, really, and no one heard me while I, Jelena's valiant Jan Hus, was holding forth:

My face is taut: I'm as erect as a pole or a cross: a real man, with a proper discharge military duties, emphatically and forever staring in the direction Jelena Belovuk exited.

....

Damn it ... is she (Jelena)—I'm the only one who's in love with her—ever going to learn why a dog that gets hit by a car doing 50 mph doesn't fly up into the air like a person, but is a lot more like a spinning vinyl record, in slow motion and getting ever slower for a long while on the ground, until it collapses; completely, without any sound whatsoever; and Jelena am I supposed to be as calm as Jan Hus was, watching the old woman bring branches for the bonfire on which he was going to be burnt? What the hell, Jelena?!

CHAPTER TWELVE

Jelena's Siamese Twin

The event is reconstructed, and then recorded in the memory of the conductor, Martin

A systematic history of Jelena's life is eluding first of all me, but it's also beyond any other person who would take up such a thankless and miserable task.

The story of the blueprint and organization of Jelena's internal and external personality! Do you think that I, Jelena's biographer, have uttered something full of wisdom with that sentence?

I meticulously recorded all that I heard come out of Jelena's lips; I have believed every word.

The other things, which have been the subject of fatuous statements by cravers and ravers, and Jelena's actual and potential lovers, believing that they're participating in the global ordering of wisdom—I have rifled through and amended those; dates, for instance, and places; I've limited their characters and unlimited Jelena Belovuk, with all of this accompanied by a feeling of the most profound obligation; bearing in mind the right that numerous people have, to interrogate Jelena.

Admittedly, at times I was guided by other motivations. Do you believe that passion in connection with duty is justified! Was it mercy ... for instance. Or on account of ontological uncertainty (whose?), killing Belovukova with a garden-variety clothesline? Her neck is thin; I know right where her jugular is; it would take just five seconds; I already calculated (tried?) it out; you yourself know that it's an attribute of mine to be precise; or chronologically exact; when I was young, I was never late for anything ...

I'm expecting (with justification) that they'll be talking about me, Jelena's biographer; and it will go like this:

THE EVENING NEWS

Murder in the Tošin Bunar District

Unidentified woman's body found at famous café
Investigation underway

The consequences of not reading the evening newspaper: the people waiting at the following bust stops: 32, 26, 20, 28, 47, 46, 704, 15, 16, 14, 36a, 36, 36b, etc., are whispering: "the guy ... that one hanging around ... over there ... sitting, holding a notebook on his knees ... cubes out of paper there he goes running away ... he wants to be a woman he's writing a biography about some girl who's a musician ... some folks are saying that she's Pergolesi's niece, but the one he's writing about is still living ... come come now, such a famous one ... unbelievable ... and a foreigner too ... and they say he goes to Pergola ... God only knows why she came here ... he tried to kill her over there you know ... there over there although ... at the Kalemegdan ... well they say no ... at the Roman well ... oh that's not possible what did he want what happened did it work … did he kill her listen to me did he kill her … ask them also twice unbelievable … but when was that … so when did it happen and what are folks saying …

I strangled her, of course. You don't believe it! You say you saw her the day before yesterday at a concert! She was very much alive. You say she was clapping, laughing, opening and closing her eyes and not sleeping, at the concert!

I am an irrefutable fact of life for her, so don't forget that factor; I finished her; I wrung her out like an orange, that red Jelena Belovuk; and I succeeded; succeeded in not becoming her past. Aren't you waiting for a bus? Aren't you exchanging whispers with the other people at the stops for bus #20 or #26? Aren't you talking about me?

My name has been recorded on her body with a cat's paw; and those lines, as you well know, extend in ten different directions; they have no beginning or end, and they are indelible.

Listen, did you read the evening paper called the *Evening News*? And … did you not see that huge font … and the rest of it … of course, and the other stuff: the obituary, the medical findings, very fresh clues in the fountain district … then perhaps a friend showed you the secret report of the municipal homicide squad?

But that's unimportant. Still, how could you really think … that she, Jelena, would be capable of … herself, you know … of finishing herself?!

Martin's story, the first part in my free arrangement, begins.

Don't believe the dates. They are arbitrary. The rest of it, I give you my word as an honorable biographer, is veracious, the same way this title is, which I am again writing down:

JELENA'S SIAMESE TWIN

the tenth of September (around midnight) 1975

Jelena's pacing around the room, catches one of her orthopedic sandals on the threshold, swings her leg around, and the sandal flies off of her foot, bounces around and lands on an ashtray, knocking it over. Jelena is cursing unintelligibly; she resumes her walking, in overdrive, as if she were preparing to exit through one of the walls, wearing a sandal on only one foot. With the toes of her bared foot she tries to pick up an unfinished cigarette from the little pile of butts and ashes on the floor. Then, hysterically (and perhaps unconvincingly), she starts giggling, sits down next to Martin and her long, white, almost shapely hand crosses the curved cushion, cupping the back of Martin's head and stroking it. All of a sudden her hand alights (like her slipper) on Martin's forehead, moves to his long nose, and pinches it! She pulls her long, white, nearly shapely hand back under the covers, simultaneously squeezing and pinching Martin's thighs, muscles, and knees. She pats his belly, scratches around his pecs, and up closer to his neck, with her hard clipped nails; Martin however doesn't move at all! With a quick jerk Jelena tilts her head, she looks at Martin and in an explosive hissing voice, the voice of a doubled-up hyena, says: *"Your skin my dear is not as rough through the sheet."*

Her spittle, in irregular sprays of drops (like for instance: twenty-nine of her miniature slippers), flies out of her mouth, and at the word *dear* comes to rest on the sheet near Martin's chin ...

I'm convinced that subsequent to that the only things he could say were this: *"Your skin is a veritable erotic mystery ... under the sheets."*

(Lest there be any perplexity here, everything had to happen just like this; but if nonetheless somebody is puzzled by Jelena's sibilant voice, you should take me quite literally; her voice has always been sibilant).

She touches the spots (presses them) where the tiny tracks of her sputum left behind moisture and she smirks ... and all at once for no apparent reason she stands up quickly (that's so like her) as if she were ashamed of her nakedness, puts on a dress and buttons it up to her neck, nervously lights a cigarette. Between two deep puffs, she flips her head of hair, turns to Martin, precisely as if I were watching, drew slowly close to his clean-shaven face (clean-shavenness is a precondition) and then she's right there next to the sharp, severed little hairs of his face. At that moment, I'm certain, she felt the conductor's uneven breathing.

Jelena slowly spelled it out: *"I'm not going to rehearsals, Martin, do you hear me, from this moment on in this room for mice and little spiders ... but not for lovers ... you're mocking me ... We'll change the way things are organized ... dammit ... but am I not the best flutist ... or maybe I'm not ... hey what's so funny I'm being serious here ... Moreover you can say that you're taking sick leave and ... why not ... that you'll call in ... Martin ... "*

Martin did not sneer! He did not open his mouth! He didn't budge!

Enthusiastically, with her finger level with her temple, Jelena explicated a concept of work, of bodily function-ings, which should start in one's fingernails and wrap up in the intestines …

Her eyes were flashed with sharp translucent beams (the way the shaving razor flashed before Martin's eyes for two or three seconds, when she, enraged, tossed it out). For no reason whatsoever Jelena (now) screams, wakes up the whole house and most likely crumples a cigarette between her index and middle finger. Why?! I'm not capable of explaining this! Anyhow, I don't be-lieve that you are worried about Jelena on account of this outlandish gesture of hers, and if you were then the best psychoanalysts in the world, several of them (as a group including you) would not succeed in explaining it or the other little details connected with Belovukova, which anyway left you perpetually chewing on your pen-cils and … peanuts?! I'm saying all of this on the teeny-weeny assumption that people believe you, at least to the same extent that filth and dust collect under Jelena's fin-gernails.

What do you think? Could Belovukova, a flutist in the orchestra of her lover, the conductor Martin, could tell him something inconceivably revolting, obscene, ugly, etc., from which the conductor would grow even more petrified. This for instance:

"Your smooth face, shaven down till it draws blood … red as a poppy … and your mother says that's from health and not from a blade … nonsense … the most important thing to have is your

mother and your health ... a true little philosopher, your mother ... ha, it's like she studies law or political science ... Martin, you are an everyday maternal maxim ... but thank god she's as wise as a unfilled bird before it gets taxidermied ... but inside in her philosophical head are swirling currents of air ... and does your mother Martin does your mother love to clean the piss off the floorboards ... which you mark every morning while you're yawning ... pure love ... mothers love everything mothers can do everything for their sons ... your mother like all the others ... your mother like all the others has fresh handy advice from her slimy uterus, out of her lap in which she rocked you when you were a baby and she dreams that you're still a sleepy little guy in her lap ... and then Martin ... do you hear me ... she pulls out like out of a well out of her dried up one after another best wishes for her child ... and she still says ... a woman can never love a man with her insides ... she always loves her only man ... only ... her son ... Martin are you deaf?!"

Of course, it's now the 10th of September already, probably two in the morning, of the year 1975!

Thus, on the 10th of September, early in the morning, in 1975, the flutist definitely stopped flipping her hair, letting (right?) her very long hair (did you know it's red) fall over her forehead, across her face, down to her waist. Her body slowly calms down. Snake-like. All the exigency in it. She trembles like a sparrow in a giant fist. Drawing close to the bed, she looks (with her blue eyes) at Martin's sleeping profile; ah, that bizarre conductor! And she says, she, Jelena, says:

"I move my hand slowly across one of the same lines on your face as on mine, with eyes closed, memorizing with the tips of my fingers the pores, fine hairs, notches, like on my own body, my own

body and face ... simultaneously, and it doesn't matter then, it doesn't, whose face it was ... it doesn't have to be yours ... thank god it need not be yours ... your face ... Martin ... anybody's ... Martin, do you hear ... anybody's ... I don't even have to know ... Martin!"

The current of thoughts spills from mouth (hers) to Martin's Adam's apple, arresting his breath:

"You're lying on me uninterruptedly, for a terribly long time ... two bodies become numb, their limbs, shoulders, necks, willing to accept proper nooses to the end, fingers like wooden dowels, mine and yours: GRADUALLY SENSE FADES, the feeling that there are two simultaneous bodies on one point ... connected. You don't say anything about this being impossible according to all the existing laws of physics! Two bodies on one point, I know how much to the sober your thoughts run! You think that geometric space cannot be violated, that a geometrical line remains untouched like a virgin, like my body here ... and your body there ... it can't be the one and the other: one has to be here and the other one there ...

You don't know Martin that without you, beyond your consciousness, it moves on to your conductor's baton, and despite the fact that you are holding it tight, it scatters, crosses the boundary, conquers the first, second, third points ... even the fourth ... simultaneously, Martin, simultaneously and therefore not one after another the baton overpowers the points, the lines of imaginary space; space is imaginary; the conductor's baton with which you direct works miracles like that, and in case you have no idea it is always BOTH HERE AND THERE, especially, Martin, especially when we're playing Dvořák's Eighth, and in the first movement my flute is putting out G-sharp, a pure Slavic triad, Slavic contemporaneousness, or better: simultaneity, and ahead to the end that way, the

*G-sharp renewing itself, strongest in that first movement, and ...
yes ... that G-sharp while the baton (yours) transcends all imaginary, there exist only imaginary, points in space, simultaneously,
Martin, my flute shapes those points ... reduces them, G-sharp
reduces the points to a single point, to one body ...*

*One body. One point, almost invisible to the members of the
audience there for the concert.*

*On top of one another, you and I, for days, that is to say for
years, if we don't move; nothing of the space remains, nothing of
our bodies would be left ... a true terrestrial comedy, but
Dvořak's symphony in G-sharp like a boomerang, like a precise
dissolution and vice-versa, counter to that ... an amalgama-
tion ... that Slavic G-sharp but in people's heads ... if we're not
in error here ... not even an abstract notion of space would be present ... in our heads ... in one of the heads ... actually in our
head there's not even the memory of space ... of heads ... of our
head ... only our confused insides (one, unitary), a mucous membrane, a smell, a giant smell that could perhaps be measured
against something gleaming that does not show up in space ... "*

In one such undivided moment, Jelena must have,
aside from wanting to pinch and touch "anybody's body
like her own," and that means outside time, noticed
Martin's motionlessness.; Martin's halted Adam's apple.

The event unfolded further at breakneck speed, that
is to say, independently and without intervention by me
of any sort:

She takes hold of his shoulder with some indeterminate intention, completely aware (unexpectedly) of the
stopped Adam's apple on his neck. He pinches his
cheeks, digs her short nails into his shoulders, tries to
pick him up, "it all resembles a joke," however, Martin

remained motionless and in her arms, a dead fish, a pretty fish out of water. She let him go. He stayed lying down, turned towards the wall, deadly serious, dead, frivolously dead from that moment on, thinks Jelena Belovuk, *"when stripping off all my clothes I lay down next to him pressing myself completely up against him, and when a hand, his hand, slid down my belly and … it stopped … it stopped right here … then … then he … he … oh god … then he died … he is dead … god but he's joking with me … he's joking yes he's joking he was playing as his hand was sliding spiderlike, tickling me … down my stomach … it wasn't joking … hand … his hand … then when it … dropped … the hand … my stomach … oh god … my stomach … my stomach."*

Deadly serious. Unseriously dead. He died scoffed at, comically. Seriously alive. Alive seriously. Stiff. Face-to-face with the wall of a room in the center of the city in a moment of transformation or sexual desire. He lived frivolously. He died seriously. Along Jelena's stomach, like down the Eiffel Tower. Height, depth, abrupt change in dimensions, and by that I mean existences; along Jelena's stomach, Martin's hand (the charms of Paris), stopped. Therefore, probably halfway (on the Eiffel Tower—an interrupted tourist itinerary—the effect is pretty sad: they no longer take tourists up the Eiffel Tower). Actually that is the only fact from his life (that he had been on the Eiffel Tower) but it was in the middle of hers—on her belly, a few steps above her belly button.

On the tenth of September, around four o'clock in the morning, 1975,

she runs out of the apartment on the fourth floor, in Majka Jevrosima Street, skipping stairs and holding her stomach, pressing energetically on it with the scorched pads of her fingertips; she turns the corner, at the consignment shop, into Nušić Street; her fingers are stuck now murderously deep (self-annihilation, the fool says) into her stomach, her mouth agape (that's universal prayer, the same fool says), the fear thereby visible on the roof and bottom of her mouth (that means: it's magnified), festering and infectious (Judgement Day, despite the prayer, the fool says).

On the tenth of September, around five o'clock in the afternoon, 1975,

the staff of the "Bosnia" restaurant saw a woman with long hair sitting "like a beggar" on the sidewalk, atop a folded issue of *Politika*, "in a lady-like way," rolling her head back and forth constantly, and she tossed her long, completely drenched hair back, violently; "her head could have flown off her neck at any moment"; she was smoking, and she threw her unfinished cigarettes away and the lit ones she crushed between her fingers; she stood up, as if she were waiting for someone, picked up the *Politika*, and thumbed through it ... several times, one after another, and then she would fold it, the newspaper, in a different way and sit down again, on the sidewalk. They said that after that, after the leafing, she sat differently, with her legs folded up under her; they say she had a bag, a big one, and from it she took "some bric-a-brac" and arranged it across the sidewalk, "she gave the cats something to eat," and the cats peered out from under the parked cars. She retreated, and all the waiters agreed that the cats weren't afraid of her; "they didn't run." They said that later on she left, leaving the *Politika* folded up there on the sidewalk. They said she pranced a little as she walked. All the waiters said: "She was wiggling … and shaking her hair … and calling out … "

On the eleventh of September, around 10 am, 1975

Martin the conductor arrived at his job. He was unable to remember all the details of the event that took place between the 9th and 10th of September. He says he thinks he had frozen up, gone rigid, that he has a few problems, that it's about his age. He said that his heart isn't quite up to snuff and that perhaps he'd had a stroke. Then he says that things don't always go right … with women, at least sometimes. He had fully incoherent memories of Jelena's screaming, of smoke, maybe a fire, and he knows that Jelena, accidentally, he says, it's definitely not deliberately, leaves a lit cigarette, it's frequent, very frequent, on the bed, in the ashtray, and that on occasion she falls asleep with a cigarette … a lit cigarette in her fingers. He doesn't know where she went when she left! When he woke up, regained consciousness, he saw she wasn't there. He remembered that they reached the apartment around 11; they had dined, he says, at the

"Lipa," and then they climbed up to the 4th floor, and he remembered that the supper didn't sit well with him and he was nauseous. He says they got undressed right away and lay down, and the final item remaining in his memory was: touching; they were touching each other, Jelena was fidgeting the entire time, and he thinks it was then that "that stroke" hit him; he did call it a stroke. He assumes that Jelena got scared and ran away somewhere, and "maybe she thought I was dead or something like that." He says he likes Jelena's mouth, which curls upward a bit but only when she laughs, or talks, or coos to him; and her neck and ears, asymmetrical, Martin the conductor called them "cosmic." He stated that those ears were the only things about Jelena that were pretty, and interesting, and attractive. For, he said, he only gets excited when he caresses the "cosmos in her ears," her lips, and sometimes, but only sometimes, her neck. He remembers that night not ... not being able to do anything. He says he kissed Jelena's "cosmic ears" in vain. Martin the conductor thinks he was stupefied by her too-white body, "gleaming and beaming, dangerous as a medusa or something ... something like a jellyfish ... from the sea ... and all of a sudden it was as if darkness were falling ... it was probably ... yes, it was fear that came over me and everything about her body seemed whiter and larger ... simply put, colossal ... " He says "that stroke" was only a defense against "the colossal, hopeless, voracious whiteness of her body."

He didn't know where Jelena could've gone. He says he asked a few people in the orchestra whether she made it there; Martin the conductor looked concerned, and very tired. He repeated timorously: "But I was dead for a while, that much is certain; I still need to get to a doctor today." He asked whether I could recommend a good cardiologist.

And what did I say in response! Surely you're asking me this out of simple, but vulgar, curiosity! Did I recommend to him some conscientious cardiologist, or a specialist in internal nightmares, torments, and man-problems? You would've (which you? And which we?) taken him right away, without wasting a minute, to that famous hospital with the doctors who are famous and kind. But what did I do for the (myocardially and internally fallen) conductor Martin, apart from holding him so that he (in the aftermath of the completed rehearsal) did not tumble into my lap—the most incapable lap on the planet—the lap of someone who writes biographies; nothing. Nothing, precisely nothing, not counting, of course, a smile, which I sympathetically sent his way. But you insist, you are unshakeable in your stubbornness, you bug me: what else, is that really all, what heartlessness! But no, I was not that stingy, and I said to him: "You don't need recommendations of any sort. You are a patently urgent case. There couldn't be anyone more urgent than you. Go by yourself, voluntarily. Anyway, people always go voluntarily to the doctor's, don't they?" I had very good intentions as I attempted to explain to him that, with regard to his heart and to doctors, and in general with all sorts of medical problems, it's not like with Jelena. Jelena leads the man who wants it and pulls the man who resists. He responded that he was familiar with that Latin maxim, and that he knew it ap-

plied to people's fates; after that, however, he unexpectedly felt better, and he announced that he'd postpone
his visit to the doctor till after, and that "for the time
being" he'd prefer to keep chatting with me. What a
goofball.

Did I push him into telling me everything about Jelena?
Everything that he thought, and everything that he
thought he knew about the love of Jelena Belovuk? I
can't say I know; he appeared to be confessing, of his
own volition, in a saintly way, his love, that is to say, his
un-love, trying to remember key things, extracting them
from his tattered and sloppy memories. I don't think I
cast any kind of spell over him; perhaps only with the fact
that he was going to become famous due to Jelena. By
dint of Jelena's disappearance. A participant. Becoming a
participant—he liked that, and how.

Martin the conductor voluntarily participated; he did
not die; he (perhaps) won't be needing a doctor, and it
looks like he has recovered his health; he (perhaps)
won't need Jelena. It seems that her departure liberated
him all right …

Right now is the perfect moment to entitle the entire
chain of events:

JELENA'S SIAMESE TWIN

Martin the conductor with love and hatred in his eyes,
on his lips in his body (not recommended by internists)
for Jelena and for the world, simultaneously, spoke for a
full two hours:

"An unusual woman! It's the same as if you were to say: an unusual color, or paint for your furniture, an oddly colored flute, piano, my baton here, my conductor's briefcase, a strange hat on a boulder of a woman an unusual tent on an unaccustomed mountain … or maybe it's like this: a noise out of the ordinary in the apartment I rented on Majka Jerosima Street, across the street from the "Bosnia," unusual curses at the "Lipa," and then the unusual deductions of the waiter from some third restaurant, unusual people, or flowers or for example: an unusual lapel in the little hole of which a flower is stuck, or a flower in a woman's hair … Imagine some unusual flower … a camelia … when would women wear such peculiar flowers as Jelena! No. Jelena didn't love flowers. She's not unusual in the least. That's all inane … I mean these singularities; perhaps she is off-beat, do you know what I mean, I'm thinking like "out of the ordinary" or "outside the norm," see?! Ugh, Jelena! I definitely don't understand in the least why she would drink … well, alcohol, I mean alcohol … she used to drink alone, too, and not just in company … if you know what I mean …

She'd call me on the phone at night, before I rented the apartment in the building across the way from the "Bosnia," and she was constantly hanging up, did this for quite a long time … You know, it used to scare my mother in particular … the telephone's in her room and she, my mother, is a tormented woman, and she's been without a husband for a long time, my father … he was a pilot … he died ages ago, when I was ten, no more than that … and Jelena, Jelena knew all of this, I told her everything about my mother, just as soon as we got going … you know, with … our … liaison, I told her all about it; but she didn't care; she rings up at night, every night, d'you see, and when she hears my mother's voice she puts down the receiver, it's unreal, my mother was simply terrified by these calls; I asked Jelena not to call, but she, just imagine what she told me: "why does your mother keep the phone in her room if she is so afraid and gets jumpy and hysterical when it rings, and why don't you move it into your room or into the foyer," imagine, I mean just image the impudence! It didn't help when I explained to her that my mother was old, almost always alone, and that the phone in her room is essential, because anything could happen ... god forbid, but she's old, you understand ... around seventy.

Listen I'll tell you something ... You know, at the start of our relationship the way she'd shake her hair really got on my nerves, you know that thing she does, I've seen other men watching, aroused ... while she ... tosses ... listen, it's like a fishing net ... You must admit it's quite unappetizing; one time I even wanted to cut off her hair ... ridiculous isn't it ... and later, later on, I also took the bait. I never asked her if she colors her hair, and she never talked to me about these cosmetic fine points ... What do you think ... so maybe Jelena didn't color her hair ... it was so light, her eyebrows and freckles were like those on natural redheads, weren't they! The fine hairs on her face and body are completely fair ... How is it that you don't know this! I got a really good look ... You can believe me!

You see, I never thought about our ... hm ... love, but it was love, one couldn't call it anything else; I mean I made not attempt to interpret, to explain ... such ... events ... now it seems to me that Jelena didn't pay much heed to me as soon as she stopped talking ... She didn't say anything about herself ... you know ... or about her parents, her friends, or about the men she loved before me and so on ... that's needed, of course ... I even think it's vital to have good talks ... but she ... nothing ... really nothing. God knows there was nothing at all! How little I know about her ... huh ... maybe you know more ... you simply understand, and maybe your methodology is also … you know, your approach … to Jelena is better … and then why am I telling you all of this, yes, why then?!"

This was the fully phony dilemma of Martin the conductor who had suddenly recovered his health and his good spirits; if you ask me, he shouldn't be believed, that is, there's no need to believe every word he says, not on account of some "methodology"—as if Jelena were an economic or social phenomenon that should be thoroughly examined, explained, exhibited to an auditorium audience in one of the big halls at the Faculty of Economics—of course not for that reason, but more because of his psychological pretensions concerning Jelena, and more than anything because Martin's love for Jelena was small, teeny-weeny like one you have for a terrier or some such creature … And Martin goes on with his story:

"She will turn up … in a day or two, I feel it, I can sense it … Smiling … ha ha you know, full of lies in that way of hers and perky … right! This isn't the first time that she has … .disappeared like this … .evaporated!

But … .just so you know … her ears so cosmic, you wouldn't have been able to notice those, with their little holes in places nobody else has them, on the upper reaches … but <u>nooo</u> those are natural holes, but what kind of earrings … what's up with you … right at the bowl-shaped parts of her auricles … barely noticeable, and therefore you didn't see them, and they are even symmetrical, the holes, in the same spots … like this, here where the ear like twists … but otherwise her ears are different … quite … .different, but you didn't see that either, and isn't that just unbelievable?"

Conductor Martin freaks out continually, despite the fact that I am exhibiting no disbelief, nor am I asking him anything, and ultimately am not even participating in his storytelling, or are those his antics, like little tricks, or is he a weirdo, or maybe he has a headache, ha ha: oh I remember: he's jealous of me.

"*I tell you, those are some cosmic ears, those little holes … yes, because of their holes … and the ears, those ears of hers are of different sizes, the left one's bigger and the one on the right is smaller, yes, smaller, and then too they were placed … the ears, I mean … I'm talking about her cosmic ears, they are positioned on a slant … one of them leans towards her face and the other one more towards the back of her head; the lower part of Jelena's left ear, you know, that little tiny place where women usually wear their earrings … well, that part is separated like a peninsula and, you know, it's really sensitive to my kisses, thank god you haven't tried that … so you don't know … it's natural for you not to know, because you don't have the same kind of relationship … as I do, you'll understand … but you're on the sidelines here, Jelena's right ear is completely insensitive, and that's simply fascinating, left-right, with her there are all these specificities, divisions, but nevertheless these cosmic fireproof ears of hers are the most beautiful things, it's just that the one on the right is insensitive to fire, I already mentioned that the right-hand one is quite unfeeling … and I tried it with a cigarette … unreal … like in an oven … you know those pans … Jelena boasted to me about it and I didn't believe it … and see, now you don't believe it either … she persuaded me to give it a go, to test it out, and so I tried it and … truly nothing … not a trace … you know it seems to me more like her ears … somehow … her essence, left sensitive, right insensitive, and the differing ways they are adjusted, one smaller the*

137

other larger ... yes double ... do you get what I mean ... she is double ... no, no, it's not being two-faced that I have in mind, but some kind of duality in everything ... Don't know how to explain it ... for crying out loud don't you get it!!

In Herceg Novi last summer, of the twenty days that we spent there, Jelena slept through at least ten of them ... she was sleeping sixteen, seventeen hours per day, like a newborn baby; she told me later in Belgrade after we'd returned that she had needed to restore her energies by means of protracted sleep, a cannon could not have woken her up, nor an earthquake, nothing! Listen, that's all a bunch of poppycock. She's just an average person with melancholy.

You know, before I rented that apartment by the "Bosnia," she was coming to see me twice a week, when my mother wasn't in the house of course. My mother cannot stand Jelena, the same way she can't stand high pressure, in the air, blood, or sudden changes in weather or Karađorđeva Street when it's stifling, my aunt on my father's side, and things like that ... so that with her it's not anything unusual, it's not hatred of any special sort, you understand, she just can't abide her ... and take me, for instance, for some reason I cannot stand the cellist ... in our ... orchestra, I mean ... so as I was saying Jelena used to come over two times a week; and one time I think this was last month, she blew into the house ... there on Karađorđeva Street, like a berserk feline ... I forget now why I hit her; it must've been because she was hiding something; she was nagging me; her nose was pointy like a snake's and she was talking, and kept on and on talking ... and my arm just suddenly flew into motion ... a man can't always control himself ... and she, well she really knows how to set you off ... and so when I hit her, she began screaming: 'Heeelp!', and I got really afraid because of the neighbors, because of my mother, she's on really good terms with them, what will they tell her and surely you *know how complicated that can get, and then it'd turn into a big scandal and my mother ... you get it it would hit her really hard I had to do something ... I shoved her up against the wall, maybe it was too hard ... I used both of my hands to stop up her mouth, you know exactly what I was trying do: she calmed down and I let her go ... and do you know what she did, then? Thank god, you could never even come up with this ... a woman like that ... sweet jesus ... she jumped on me ... yeah, she sprang onto me ... started scratching me hysterically ... she had completely lost her mind, that was the moment ... when I went off the deep end I shook her ... Now I regret it I was sorry about it right away ... the blood was running out of her nose ... but damn what are you supposed to do with her when she's hysterical ... and after that it was total madness, good god, she lost her mind, went insane, yeah, she was bananas ... all kinds of things could've happened ... it could have gone down even worse ... well, what happened, she threw all the dishes out the window in the kitchen, and then she laid hands on the cabinet made of oak, my mother's dowry ... when she married my father, she brought that cabinet into the household, since then, and especially since his death she's taken really good care of it, you understand that kind of sentimental connectedness to objects ... and Jelena knew all of that, I know ... it was a fit of rage ... I understand ... probably she didn't mean to ... but anyway she destroyed it ... the cabinet, I mean, with a knife, with some knife or other that all of a sudden found its way into her hand ... oh god ... I'll never forget it ... and that, why are you pretending that you don't understand, that crazed look in her eyes ... that's when I grasped everything, everything ... she was yelling something like: "And dressers live longer than we do repulsive idiotic things objects that should be destroyed systematically, methodically like with this knife' and she was brandishing it at me, it was so messed up, she would've ... she was going to why the hell can't you see this ... in that kind of rage she was capable of killing someone and ... you know ... then ... that day while she was hopping around, what do you mean who, it's Jelena ... jesus haven't I been telling you about Jelena this whole time obviously it hasn't been about my mother or your wife ... you say you aren't married no matter it's insignificant, it's not important ... besides, what do I care about your wife or your non-wife ... I was telling you how Jelena was leaping around like an unbridled filly ... you don't think a filly can stampede?! And stop it already, looking at me all suspicious, I can't figure out why you're always ogling me, and you don't have to constantly and I mean constantly look me in the eyes ... you're wrecking my concentration ... and you interrupted my sentence with your ... well ... your conspicuous glaring fine, okay, I know you didn't mean anything by it ... there it is again ... can't you get it through your head, for god's sake, that your eyes ... those eyes of yours ... I don't like them, you're all bug-eyed, dammit, just don't let your corneas slip out, but hey your eyes are also a weird color ... that's better ... the walls are better, you know they're more neutral than my face ... while I'm talking ... about Jelena ... please don't turn around ... don't look at me, now I can continue; I was telling you about that day when she was bouncing around on the "things that outlive us" like an unbridled filly, I was straining to think of what my mother's reaction would be when she caught sight of her violated world, you understand, that oaken cabinet was her whole entire world ... she owed her life plain and simple to that piece of furniture ... to some mementos that were in the drawers ... what I have in mind are letters and little things like that ... she destroyed everything ... cardboard boxes with photographs and letters, some brochures that were in the boxes to ... tore them up ...*

good god, how I hated her then, in those seconds ... and train tickets, my parents' ... their honeymoon, and just so you know what a piece of shit that Jelena is, my father's handkerchiefs had been ironed and neatly arranged in the top drawer by my mother, and Jelena pulled them out one after another and used them all to wipe her shoes, her soles ... nothing but mud ... on her shoes ... I could have ... I could've and I give you my word of honor killed her then ... with pleasure ... flat-out enjoying ... yes, yes ... killing her ... but I didn't lay a finger on her, you know, all at once that fury in me abated like dust somehow ... like when dust settles ... and by and by, by and by I threw her out of my house; she wasn't seen for a month; nowhere, nowhere at all; didn't even show up for rehearsals, and we had to find a replacement for her ... but then ... then I, you know, found out her address and of course I asked her, I asked her to come back, she demanded that I rent an apartment ... that's how it started ... What do you mean, what?! For crying out loud ... our ... relationship.

Dammit didn't I tell you not to look at me, I ... I simply can't bear it ... I love her ... I definitely love her, there's nothing odd in that, and I told you it wasn't weird and why, why did you turn your head back around just now, listen ... if I ask you something ... it's not important, never mind, I can see it doesn't interest you ... it's irrelevant really!

But you know, my mother took an eternal dislike to Jelena even though I took part of the fault for the ruined things on myself; my mother never even got to know Jelena, but when Jelena would come by now and again, my mother would draw certain conclusions about her person. I could never establish, for instance, by what means she decided that Jelena was slovenly! She has her codes, her rules, mechanisms, and she says that she doesn't have to lay eyes on a person, but if he or she has spent at least an hour in her

*house, she can infer all kinds of things … by means of these
markers of hers … I don't even know what they are, but still you
can assume they were the same old bullshit … in the majority of
cases it had to do with hygiene or orderliness, for example, you
see … but those aren't identities, and I tell her that. She decided
that my Jelena is a slob … oh mother my mother … but that's all
hogwash right?! Don't you think so as well … and that hygiene,
neatness, things in their place, shoes polished, laces tied, shirts
ironed, bed made tight … creases on pants, socks the same color as
the pants, hair brushed, perfume and things I won't continue to list
tell me … do you agree that this is bullshit … that it's all a tire-
some bother, fine, you don't have to say but I can see it … your
shoes don't shine, the creases on your trousers are nonexistent, ha,
and your hair is disheveled, plus maybe you haven't bathed for
several days! We're definitely of one mind on this … I can feel
it … I don't have to see trivial things … I sense them like she
does, my mother … I feel them in advance, before I see them!*

*And if I tell you that she decided Jelena was slovenly, you see,
there was no intuition in it, it was pure empiricism yeah yeah, it's
very simple but no matter she was not right; Jelena left full ash-
trays all around the apartment, and then too glasses we had used
for wine, you know we drank wine more than anything, she usually didn't wash them, and when she did wash them she didn't
turn them over to dry, plus, after taking a bath she didn't clean
the bug, she left newspapers spread out on the kitchen table, unwashed plates if we happened to eat lunch there, in my mother's
apartment … things like that … I tried to talk my mother out of
it, I claimed we'd been in a rush, but nothing worked; I told her
that Jelena was smart and as hardworking as she could be, that
she was the greatest flutist but that ultimately that didn't matter
because she wasn't stuck-up … but the, however much I'd wanted*

for her to accept Jelena, or at least to quit hating her, at some point I accepted the fact that Jelena was right; you get it ... it's not totally bad if you sometimes throw dishes out the window, rip up photos "methodically," see ... not out of rage ... with utter calm ... destroy a few more of my mother's relics ... by calculation ... liberate her from her obsessions and put on her lifelong loathing for you like you would a coat ... plus her loathing could be shed like a coat, too ... in the springtime. And Jelena? Jelena was still my wise busy little bee ... She'll come back ... she'll come back I know it, this isn't the first time ... I know ... soon; about my mother she said that she's a frustrated woman and would surely become a sex maniac if we were to live twice as long as we're going to live, it would take her that much time to forget my father, Jelena says, she'd need that much time to become a woman again, even if a maniacal one, she'd be a woman, and then you can imagine, Jelena concluded: since we will not live that long, she, my mother, will take to her grave with her a body pledged to her husband, her first and only man, my late father; but it doesn't matter ... that ... these things relating to my mother ... it really does not matter!

You know, Jelena ... Jelena loved ... Jelena loved to be touched ... for somebody, anybody, to touch her ... understand: her body, her lips, always the lips, her tongue, multiple complex embraces, cheek-pinching, feet ... whatever ... everywhere, in every place, at any moment, she could, she really could twenty-four hours a day ... be touched, you get it, it was irrelevant whose hand was stroking her hair, her face ... and you see it was of no consequence which part of the body ... hers ... she, you know experienced things very strangely ... her body ... as if she didn't share it ... as if ... do you get it?! I like that ... it could be taken as tenderness, don't you think?

143

And she told me how an elevated frequency of touches lets us free ourselves from the loneliness of the animals … She was thinking, most likely, of physical loneliness, you know … I'm betting you've felt this at least once yourself … the nonexistence of "the other," actually "the other me" … but not because of that, it's all in the physical sense … do you follow … the meaning of this is the Greek word, physis, nature … these are Jelena's ideas … everything relates to the body … to the nonexistence of another body right next to me hard by me that could be like this body of mine … but it's not because of that, that's not the reason why she can't tell herself for sure that she exists … I don't know that she has ever said that, but I do know she thinks that way … she thinks that she isn't sure she exists … and she has said that she would've been happy to be born as a Siamese twin … this sounds crazy … right?! Another body next to her, another Jelena, double Jelena … it's all the same: needs, thoughts, wishes, sicknesses; everything two-fold; twice the death, twice the appetite for men … what kind of guy would sleep with Siamese twins?! Good Lord … Can't get my mind around it … I just can't … plus it's disgusting … and this desire of hers to be glued to another identical body which could … you know … think the same thoughts … she would die that way with someone else … but in actuality alone with herself … the other body would be neither totally hers nor totally someone else's … dear god … she senses in that a chance for her beingness, security … you don't believe it?! Then you don't know her well enough anyhow … and with you she certainly didn't … talk about things like this … Yeah, and she couldn't have … I doubt that you got together that many times with her … I'll admit I wasn't even with her every day … but still … nonetheless don't you get it!?

Once, you know, I observed her while I was concealed behind a parked car, in a half-crouch; she was at a bus station, here by the

*economics faculty; just so you know, just so you can see how flirty
she was with her boyish looks, with her girlish figure, for instance;
her rolled-down patterned kneesocks, her wide wrinkled skirt,
barrettes in her hair and stuff like that; and she was wearing a
huge sweater and ... smoking ... yes on the street ... she wasn't
pretty and she wasn't ugly, simply nice-looking, somehow girl-next-
door-ish ... but those legs of hers ... those legs alone, it was all
about the legs, her figure and ... the freckles ... the freckles on her
nose.*

*Other people were observing her stealthily, like me; that's when
I felt jealous ... and I couldn't hold back ... from behind the
car ... I leapt out in ambush ... and it was an ambush, you'll
understand, all of a sudden, from out of nowhere, I materialized
right next to her, my Jelena with the plastic barrettes in her tangly
unbrushed hair. She sneered; she suppressed a guffaw; but she
wasn't surprised in the least ... as if she'd known, as if she'd seen
me!? Ugh, Jelena ... just be aware ... you cannot deceive her in
any way ... she, you see, has an ability to sniff things out ... she
simply senses ... feels in advance. Ugh, Jelena! It's like the red
plush on the seats in the theater ... but with the rivets tar-
nished ... copper ones ... Don't you follow?! You really don't
understand?! Well then you really truly don't know her.*

*She will come, I'm not worried about it at all, I'm doing fine
here now, huh, I could do a little dance, things are going that well
for me; I'm certain that she will come, maybe even today ... if not
because of that other stuff then at least to pick up from the apartment ... there, opposite the "Bosnia," her slippers, and odds and
ends of that sort ... well fine, she could go purchase those ...
right ... but her music notebooks ... she'd have to ... she'd need
to at least for the sheet music ... You understand ... she can't
obtain sheet music all that easily ... You don't agree?! Naturally*

I am not worried, look at the way I just lit a cigarette, now that's a heart for you. Come on now, I feel young … There's nothing wrong with me … it was a passing phase, but now what pluck, what doctors, what's wrong with you!? I feel it's my thousandth sense, hereditary, like with my mother, I can feel that she will come, and earlier she'd leave unexpectedly but you see she'd come back, usually, with a bouquet of irises, not always … for my mother … my mother had an uncommon love of irises, and Jelena will come back with irises … I feel it … I even see it … perhaps any moment, if I tell you that by tonight … by tonight she'll be here, smiling and lying … you don't believe it?! What do I care. You don't have to!

CHAPTER THIRTEEN

Jelena's Second Letter

I crossed a space of several thousand kilometers; however, the actual distance is null; I never took off at all!

Parameters of the event (the changes): 2 o'clock in the morning; the elevation of the 4th floor (the ferry); below is black plasma (the sea).

My dear M , what's below this huge slow ferry is sea, and naturally it has no link of any kind to the deepest of hatreds that I feel towards you just now, but on that account my hatred is not also accidental or arbitrary or a momentary caprice of my emotional being. Because of everything that exists between the two of us, it's obvious that you know what's going on with me! I could, with an utterly clear conscience, entertain the thought that you M are responsible for all of this; and that I, ignorant of the events in which I am participating so sparingly, am the motive, the main motivation of your personality ... for these ... perverse and stupid, above all stupid ... objectives.

My dear M , I hate you with all my strength; that is isn't it, as if I had said: I love you with all my strength, since those impossible and fictitious intensities cancel each other out; imagine now: pure indifference; after everything! I do not doubt that you're already asking, as dull-wittedly as ever: 'But ... after what ... what happened ... and ... owing to what exactly?'

Experiment:

I enter a men's toilet (just now)—no one sees, nobody is watching; I go in again; and: *"in a world of options, in a world of thrift"* (I'll bet you ten pieces of marzipan that when I return you won't know who wrote those lines in English!) and on the ferry "Virginia," the metal intestines of which I am living through sentimentally, as if it were a matter of a very large hot woman, sailors (five of them) and travelers (one woman, four men, and a child), with crew cuts and faces clean-shaven (the male element) hysterically to the point of redness, tidily like their lawns too, staring stunned at my figure-little body that emerged not bashfully in the least out of the bathroom facilities set aside strictly for men.

To me it seems like I dreamt about this harbor ... something similar to this ferry ... several nights back, or more, maybe even all of thirty nights back!? And ... the dream ... I put it down ... the dream ...

A waiting room planted on the water like a fat woman in a chair; that's the first image; can you M imagine this with that thick head of yours? An empty waiting room with benches reminds me of a terrace with a stone railing, on the water, like at the sea ... in some small town.

The second image is the filling up of that waiting room: me, in a group of fifty people, disembarking from the ship, which suddenly presses up against the railing (before this it wasn't there at all); everyone jumps over the railing, we have our carry-ons in our hands; we're lightly dressed, like for July or August; I recognize the late Anton; I see that he has a long beard, glasses, a somewhat longer nose than he actually had; and beyond that checked pants like an American, a name-tag on his shirt pocket—indicating membership in a tourist group that's traveling around the globe, a yellow cap on which is written in English in block letters: "I am a failure"—a wisecrack, like a warning to hotel staff, waiters, airport and the ship's crew, and merchants. Among the travelers I also see my nonexistent father! How do I know it's him? I have never seen him, nor in my dream had he aged. He's a little stiff; probably by dint of his having arrived in the dream (memory) directly from a photograph! He has on the same clothes ... his body's in the same position ... as in the photo ... He's not moving! A pair of men is sticking close by him ... They're holding him by the elbows; he, my father, looks like he isn't alive! But Anton, Anton has, imagine, changed his appearance and his nationality; he has learned English and gotten rich in the meantime; and maybe he has gotten married, there, in America!

You I did not see ... You need not believe that and I don't give a damn. Incidentally, I do not always dream of you! But there, in my dream, amidst the passengers, was Professor Rodić. Upon a signal of some sort, it is likely that a signal existed, maybe a siren to signal danger or a cloudburst (the waiting room had no roof), we all started jumping into the water. I say "started," because ... it lasted a while ... it was jumping, not a jump, gradual and slow; we were jumping with our noses held; in one hand our satchels, in the other: our nostrils fused and held by our thumbs and index fingers. Again you can't believe it! You are suspicious even of my dreams, as if I had a reason to deceive you with something in a dream of my own? As if I were at all capable of deceiving you? You controlled me perfectly, unerringly, M , absolutely infallibly; bullshit! So of course we were jumping into the water holding our bags and our noses! Anyway, that's a completely normal thing even in daytime ... You don't have to believe it, don't have to contort your pointy face, ... you don't have to do anything, you don't have to, my M , not even to read this letter, you can tear it up, in the same instant the mailman delivers it to you (I'm sending it by registered mail), before his very eyes, just to confuse him!

Listen M , the precondition for my going on with this letter is your unconditional, absolute and definitive belief in every one of my words, in each of my commas, exclamation points, spaces, breaks, in all of my grammatical mistakes, in all my chicken scratch, because nothing is accidental ... not a single little dot ... in every letter M , even when you suspect (this will certainly occur) whether the letter is intended for a different person, some other M ; for some person who has the same number of letters in his or her name as you do, M , and whose name begins with the letter M.

Things interrelate, continue, and elaborate on themselves to each other only when they occur simultaneously. A dream, a crossing of the English Channel. The sea, the canal, the ferry that rocks..as I am writing this, the other travelers are reading or napping, here, in the restaurant, because no one wants to pay extra for a cabin, provided otherwise, only for the ship's crew.

I am #11 on board this ship, if I include only the adults. It's like a beginning, that number eleven! After ten you start with the singles; that's the beginning for me. I, my own beginning, to my own self.

I am starting, something, different, do you understand M ! Incidentally always when it begins, something else is at stake, that difference goes without saying; it is, however, as I said: I am not starting, at all, not anything. Nonsense! Starting all kinds of things! And you see, I equated my life with an unspecified action; however I might label that action, you while you are reading and I while I am writing and once more me while I renew myself; that is in fact a physiological function: the swaying of the ship = the ship; barking = the dog = Maša's dachshund; Jelena = Jelena's beginning = the new Jelena = your decision; and so on down the line ...

I told you: we were leaping into the water with our bags, clutching our noses; from out of the water we bubbled up, or perhaps we swam, slithered?! I don't know; through some hallways; they resembled ... the passageways into catacombs, a pharaohs' refuges, the basements of pyramids (do these exist?) in which are kept the bodies of the best servants, female lovers, male lovers, blacksmiths, locksmiths, manservants, carpenters, guards, and seamstresses (someone, I guess, had to sew all those robes for them).

All right, all right; you don't have to say anything at all ... but I see already, I already see, M , how you're raising your left eyebrow pressing your lips together, you crumple up this piece of paper … you don't know what it might … you're perplexed (are you surprised?) … in anger you light a cigarette and then immediately stub it out!

You will think to yourself: "Look, she wrote in the name of her deceased uncle right down to the last letter, and she was not even especially close to him … and in the name of Maša's dachshund, and the whole entire name of some lousy ship on which that bitch is running around shaking her booty, down to the last letter, and other names … but me she categorizes me with a vague letter 'M' … what a petty little act of revenge!

I go on with the letter with an enormous effort to set forth things with some degree of orderliness; if however you notice some confusion, my most faithful M , in the world, then either things have transpired chaotically or the confusion is in your head!

You were always, M , pedantic! Why would I avenge myself on you like that, abbreviating your name (and you obtusely believe it's you, to boot) down to one letter! That's insufficient by the way; abbreviating your name, here, in this place, not near the seashore not far off, do you understand M ? In the middle of the trip, which was, certainly, mine but … by your decision; as if I were abbreviating you, repressing … so that's why it resembles revenge, because in me, you will believe, remains the indeterminacy of the letter "M" that could with time become the initial letter of someone else's, but not your, name! It's cockeyed but funny to think about in that vein. It could happen that in my memory I'm hanging on to several "M's" and that not a one of them will be yours ... your name; nevertheless another possibility exists also; every letter M might stand for an adjective in front of your name.

My little M , I have by no means sworn off revenge! I have never waived revenge! I have no doubt that these are small, sweet joys, and that they are abhorrent, witless, slimy, etc.; I'll allow you such an impression. I wanted at one time to explicate revenge to you as a gesture, a long-lasting gesture; with something from inside that you would have to feel just as I do; as if you were me! It felt odd to watch you; I was watching myself; your face was mine, your long legs, still long, were also mine; your flat feet and fatigue; and that dumb shit now and then, at the conservatory, like before anesthesia or directly after it; a consciousness erased in a drastically simplified process; a vacuum that causes physical pain, when your stomach is touched or your throat but more so your stomach. You said, once: "It must be ... that Anton died that way, similarly ... It has to be that that's just the way people die, generally speaking ... do you understand Jelče ... like that ... vacuumed up like before an abortion, by the hand of death—the hand of the anesthesiologist ... Anton, that weirdo uncle of yours felt the momentary sting, don't you think it was like that ... the needle held by a man who knows something about veins, right? With the hand, of the man, who understands veins, presses itself, just like that ... pushes itself into ... the stuff from inside, which was amassed and concentrated outside, into the stuff that is scattered and indefinite, like dust, like dust!"

Those were literally your words; you cannot now, or at any future date, deny that you said that; and you cannot accuse me of lies and nonsense ...

I started to write you about my dream, but my secret thoughts ... oh, my secret desires made of this letter, of these sentences—a screed about revenge, raving in secret ... but all of it is your fault ... You set all of this in motion! It should be otherwise: everything that's in the brain (my head or yours, no matter) that's connected with this, should be encircled and separated from the rest, there should be a place in the brain that's wiped clean, right before our eyes as it were; first observe and then palpate, and then from the central source of its strength and capacities peel it away, tighten the noose with its peripheral powers around the arteries of vindictiveness and: strangle it! The eagle that clenches the snake! That's how it should be! What a coward I am! I still have not made a plan, for the irrevocable jump, a snake-like jump, you know, and it's like I have given up/changed my mind ... owing to tradition ... owing to some like moral imperatives or owing to some laughable sense of refinement, because of that: "it's not nice"?!

But, my M , don't rejoice prematurely at our similarity. There's rhyme and reason to it, one single reason; and that is because, if something happens, not "something" but that pure deed if my viper stings you right between the eyes, that is to say, at the spot where hairy personage eyebrows meet up, it will occur precisely because of the similarity between you and me ...

I should at this point go on with the dream. I stopped when we were jumping into the water ... and then the passage through the cellars of pyramids, then the return, intriguingly ... in this moment one of the travelers ... accidentally ... by accident touches me, he reached out for the newspaper on the table, while he was picking it up, he touched me; we came back from the basement by the steps that were covered in slick skin ... like a membrane; we hooked our fingers, fingernails into the slimy covering, grabbed on to one another and somehow reached the waiting room. The journey through water and sewer tunnels repeated itself ... several times. After every jumping there were fewer of us in the waiting room; before we jumped into the water the final time, some people showed up dressed in white doctors' coats with cartons of some kind of fat in their hands; I think there were five or six of us; the people in the white coats stripped us naked but we didn't resist; and they vigorously rubbed us down with salve; and our hair as well as our faces, and then they disappeared the same way they had turned up.

That passenger now returned the newspaper to the table; I saw his hand ... puffy, broad ... probably strong enough, probably strong enough to cup my distended belly, to squeeze my stomach, but I didn't raise my eyes. I even tipped my head down farther; in that way, I managed to keep only his hand in my field of vision, the exciting hand of an otherwise perhaps utterly uninteresting man?!

And in the dream: there remained on the platform only the late Anton, an unknown man from his tourist group, both of them wearing caps and little badges, and me: therefore only three of us prevailed over all of the traps that my "I who dream" had so maliciously set. The end is brutal; my deceased uncle Anton does not even in my dream stay alive; the "I who dream" isn't able to escape from the tyranny of actual events; or, as you would put it, M : it's sending information via the fastest telegraph in the world, "I who do not dream."

The ship appears; the waiting area—platform gets a roof and benches; the unknown man from Anton's "I am a failure" group pulls some papers out of his travel bag that he curiously didn't lose in the water or in those icky corridors we have to wriggle through; from out of the ship emerge these big mustache men wearing the uniforms of our traffic cops; my late uncle Anton, as it happens, does not recognize me in the dream, he suddenly (isn't that perfect: suddenly) he starts to scream ... it's not even human, at first his shrieks reminded me of a ship's horn, and they lasted, well ... maybe a minute, certainly no longer, and then he toppled over onto the floor of the waiting room; that "I am a failure" colleague of his walked towards the boat and thrust (all at once) into the hands of one of the traffic policemen all the papers that he had a moment before removed from his bag. How it looks when in a dream panic begins to carry the day: a man enters the ship, the cookie-dusters (both of them) study me, questioningly; and of course right then I see that I have lost my travel bag with all my documents and my return ticket on the occasion of the jumping; and what am I doing ... I am trying to board the ship with brute force, nothing doing, my strength is laughable, negligible; the ship departs, I return to my bench covered in tears like in the best, most severe attacks of hysteria from earlier in my life, with my stomach cramping up … from fear!!??

The cramps in my stomach woke me up … They're unreal, and I don't know how I managed to endure them … to withstand such pains!

"The onset of madness," you say, or perhaps, idiotically as ever, "you should wait for another ship … surely one will come dock … in the dream … in your dream, Jelena … or some other means of transportation!"

Am I to break off this letter because a possible commentary-thought (yours simultaneously as it is mine) has emerged as the most grievous insult?!

Does it make sense, dear M , for me to write you, if you respond to the cramps in my stomach called forth by a distressing dream with: "the onset of madness!" ? Or, I mean, is it a matter of complete indifference if I also say: "the onset of madness."

For other reasons I'm going to give up on writing for a while.

The ship's clock read 4 pm!

I ate the toughest schnitzel of my life; vegetables: blades of grass, green-and-white, resembling clover, peas from a can; white wine; my life forces returned, measured in degrees on the scale of Mr. Celsius, my vitality (at this moment) is somewhere around seven clicks above zero. Am I glad about this thaw? Am I of sufficiently sound limb to be capable of withstanding uninterrupted travel without pain my joints, feet, calves, and hips? My spine. My dear M , I have a sick spine and a sick liver in which all the neuroses of this world, into which precipitate; but aren't travelers just like that? – I've seen that some have blue eye sockets, sweaty palms, and greasy, greasy foreheads; tell me, M , doesn't it seem to you too that people who travel have to have shaved heads, because of the wind, and also because of the varied and multi-colored headgear ... and ... you see ... like Tsvetaeva ... travelers!

I powdered my nose and forehead in the bathroom, once again, the men's; I didn't wash my hands, I did not blow my nose, and I did not put Shanida by Yardley behind my ears ... or anywhere else, not on a single place on my body. I didn't dab Shanida here and there so I'm dirty and I stink, like a pole-cat ... but then aren't all travelers smelly?

What a fantastic decision: I'll pay extra for a cabin; I'm expecting the ruddy-faced boss not to take the money, since at the most it's only twenty more minutes to Dover; but I would be able to get a touch more sleep; it would also turn out to be more than twenty minutes ... Maybe as much as forty, while the ferry drops anchor and while they unload automobiles and other things ... So what do you think?

Ha! Pure craftiness of mind ... so to speak ...

And in the cabin ... and in my vagina ... listen, dearest M , a man built almost like the Renaissance tumbled into my life ... into my cabin; not a single scalawag anywhere on the seas is as decisive and drunk as this medieval knight ... and you, I know it already, are asking, you're keeling over with curiosity, what happened in the cabin in the middle of the sea, to me, or to you, why not, maybe to you too?

Aha, so there we go! You will have to wait a while longer: but until then, just so you know, your Jelena is hanging out on the dock like it's her own flank (I mean my hip) and in Dover; I'm not jumping around here, this letter isn't geography or history either like back in school, d'you remember … You aren't allowed to skip things … and besides why would I write this much if I could do it shorter; and you think: but hey, it can't be any shorter!

It's totally clear to me what kind of sad position you find yourself in as you're reading this … You're already reading! But despite your jaded sentiments, which I would have to tart up with a description of the goings-on in that enchanted cabin or magical vagina (you always insisted on exact and concrete information about the genesis, duration, and form of orgasms), as if I'm narrating it to myself (without any desire whatsoever to make myself or you laugh), this that I'm going to relate to you will have, I believe, a different effect!

The man, the scalawag, this drunk, and who knows what all else he is, who bewitched me with his entry into the ship's cabin and with his proximity (it was more than sensory) just now left to go buy tickets for both of us.

I'm continuing the journey well supplied with fire in my finger-tips and a light but dangerous tremor.

"But what actually happened in the cabin," you ask, totally losing your patience already. Well it's like this: undeniable is the fact that he got into my cabin forcibly; he shoved the door with all his strength and it slammed against the iron edge of the bed frame on which I lay, half-clothed and half-asleep; then a shoe, his, whizzed

159

past my nose, or as it seemed to me, just past my nostril; then his wooden suitcase (ridiculous: a wooden suitcase) fell with a crash from the upper berth; by the way, the cabin contained two beds, with one placed on top of the other. I was on the ground floor; when my fellow traveler's suitcase fell, I stood up and shoved it with my foot. I was barefoot and in my undershirt, ("Already" you ask), and holding myself upright, probably while making a furious face, I stared at him. You're croaking from the anguish now, you big jerk … M , you're a bitch, and I know the way you're grinning and taunting me now. He mumbled something, and, I assume with the intention of apologizing, he jumped off of his bed, but could he have been any clumsier? Since I was standing right by the edge of the bed, he could jump either onto me or into the window, or like onto the sink at the opposite end of the room; none of this was especially convenient, that is, comfortable, for my fellow traveler; incidentally, this was an fraction of a second, a nebulous decision in his head. Naturally you already know—you aren't that dumb: *he jumped on me, yep, right onto me, but M , if you don't stop smirking, you absolutely will not get to hear the part that interests you the most!*

Above all, it wasn't intentional, although you think it was. For me to be standing there right by the edge of the bed, as I've already told you—but motivation? He could have had ulterior motives … for … his … jump. Nonetheless, that's not important … it was unavoidable; he fell on me like a tree; I staggered under his weight and I almost found myself on the floor of the cabin when I felt his arms firmly gripping my back; it was an

160

impossible position, fully contrary to the law of physics: the entire weight, my entire weight, shifted to his center of gravity, he had picked me up off the floor and bracing his legs held me like that for several minutes; then when he lowered his hands, we remained pressed together, along the length of my thighs. Ah you ... M , you ... with your brainless questions: "What did that guy look like ... were his arms that long, maybe he was shaped like a monkey, his body; I mean, could his arms since he could reach down (my) (not your) thighs hang even lower ... below his knees?"

I'm not gonna tell you anything! Not his ethnicity, nationality ... not the first letter of his name ... never, never will I utter such in front of you. What do you care, anyway, what his name is, who he is, where he's from, what he does for a living, how much money he has, whether he's poor, what he's doing, why he's crossing the English Channel and why is he traveling on past Dover with me!

And if I were to relate all of that to you, on the condition that I know it wouldn't be of any use. You would, my divine M , forget all of this in the twinkling of an eye, before you could smoke one of your "Drinas," filterless; or let's say to the extent that you remember something from out of the great amount of data, you would make, skillfully, I don't doubt, your own version of this even and over time (once more, lickety-split—and that is time) give in to the conceit that it happened to you, the Channel at your back; red-tired passengers; the ferry "Virginia"; a drawing of Queen Victoria above the sink in the men's bathroom, naked on a toilet, with her holding on her lap a pedantic little prime minister, you just saw that, you, you went alone into the men's toilets, of course it was you, you were just now writing about it, you and not me, and so on down the line M ; gigantic birds shriek and dive, here somewhere in the vicinity. I don't see them. My fellow traveler and future lover (right?) is still standing in line, leafing through a news-paper and not turning his head (his glance) in my direc-tion; Pardon M , your fellow traveler and your current lover! Your beginning, your orgasmic spasm because of the black plasma sea, early of a morning; it's your every-thing, M . Not in the furthest reach of my mind would I cast doubt on such an equation. I believe, moreover, that all of this is happening to you and I'm just noting it down. I'm typing out innumerable little dots, marks, codes on long, narrow pieces of paper for all possible future interpretations!

These people truly are red in the face! And you don't skip that part when you tell it!

And the serve, on offense? How many moments or even how many minutes have to pass before that blow with a level, concentrated swing, fierce and lightning-fast and of course unerring!?

What is the placement of the wrist on the occasion of such a precise serve, M ? Can it be even a little bit, an extremely small amount, twisted?!

To all appearances my traveling companion bought the ticket; he walked towards me with powerful steps; I really don't know who he is; I also don't know where he and I are going. Would you, M , ask your parachutist: "Where are we going?" Or would you, perhaps, ask me, while you are sleeping now (with whom?) at this moment, and dreaming, probably dreaming (it is six in the morning), perhaps with just a bit of viciousness: "Where are you traveling with this guy, Jelena?" Or, or ... or will you after you read this letter sound the alarm publicly: "Jelena is traveling around Europe in the company of an unknown man who the hell knows what all he might do to her."

He's here! I have to go M , I'll continue this letter later ...

the next day

meantime ... What all has been happening in the meantime?! Listen M , all kinds of thoughts have been milling about in my head; this man, I can feel it, is necessary for me; he is so necessary, that the very thought of pulling ... from that, as we always said, jointly, *"Getting rid of someone else's breath on your own face would not liberate the horizon, the range of your own breathing,"* then I would have to do something violent, like this trip is in fact violent, it seems to me; but how pathetic! We're saying, aren't we, both but not at the same time. However, I would have to write down the date ... the time ... the city, and where I found myself, etc., etc., on the huge warm lip of this unknown man, M . But the address, why don't you just write that here even if you've lost everything? I really would have to ... that address ... but in the next letter; in the next letter M , I will bring you up to date on all the decisions connected with the rough stuff in Europe, ha ha ... and I will send you a photo of this guy (if he wants to give me one), if it's necessary to placate Aunt Maša (she will, I know, seek through Interpol an acknowledgement of the paternity of her future grandchild); it's mandatory that the address be on the back of the envelope; M , I'm going to do everything because of you, if it ever occurs to you to ask my parachutist anything about me (o iniquity!), the way I would, in some convenient moment of life, ask him about myself or about you! Just so you know M : there's absolutely no need for you to spread around the news of my "strange" letter or the "strange or "delusional," that is, disordered thoughts in "that" letter, for even if we remove (the two of us teases) or (my guy and me) the possibility of confusion in the letter and confusion in your head, then with no doubt whatsoever there remains the fact (conclusion) that you cannot understand all of this toil and intrigue, just as you cannot understand: why in Rhodesia ... "Christians are afraid of pagans," like you cannot understand (because you are incorrigibly dumb) why one must kiss dogs and cats on the snout; and also M , believe me, never, absolutely never will you grasp why one must slice one's veins a few moments before climaxing (mutually) ... jointly cutting veins and in such a calculating way that the blood slips away at the same time, definitely, when through both sets of sexual organs orgasm, sweeps tingling downward, forever!

You will, M , I know, die "on time" and "legally" since you are scared to death of cars, planes, trains, ships, and so on down the line; as far as I know, you never take trips anywhere, you never drive, you never leave a place without advance traffic and weather reports and you are totally happy with your satisfied and wrecked insides, how many times have they been destroyed, with your long legs that always stretch out in one direction, very carefully (you walk and you fuck; you fuck and you walk—it's the exact same); and never in the other more important direction, or in a third unknown one! M, no one will ever kill you; you are going to die (for heaven's sake, you have to!) at a very advanced age according to the forces and laws of nature; and don't go announcing now, you fool, that I want to kill myself!

If you go to see Masa, don't take her this letter; you can only tell her, Masa, that I am fine and that I don't miss anyone or anything, except for her; furthermore I give you permission to kiss the crap out of her on both cheeks in my stead!

... mutual suicide—there exist dear M books about it; maybe also detailed instructions about how best to do it or how to attempt it but remain alive; and consequently you can't think that lunatic ideas emerge from my head only ...

... it's truly fortunate that there are as many crazy people as there are normal ones (a division that you embrace, and which the normal we or they adopt, like doctors – idiots – shrinks in Nazi gas vans, buffoons, employers in Europe, black marketeers in Czechoslovakia) but the priests are much much better ... isn't that right ... you ... dumb broad you always think the same thing ... always the same as me ... and then and then when in your head there is not one single thought, and then when you sleep and don't dream and don't dream about anything right, well, thank God that it's better to choose priests than doctors ... in these conditions thank God also that priests exist ...

what day is it in order since I left

M, you will know better; actually, you already know; you calculated it, a simple mathematical act, you did not require a Digitron, and you also don't have one; you could (you already have) in the wink of an eye with the help of the fingers on your left and right hands a few times over; and while I copy out the most nonsensical message (because you won't understand it) in the world, you know exactly how long I've been absent ... but enough about time; what's it to me, time, what the hell ...

hotel

Another night has passed; I see your eyes open wide M , right, you're following the main event ... and you know ... so read on and be disgusted:

At the front desk of the hotel we handed over our passports, got a key in the same instant, so to speak, without the customary and unpleasant procedures and looks that of bewilderment or curiosity that follow all travelers-unexpected guests (after the renting of a room with a single bed) from the front desk to the stairs or the elevator.

We did not exchange a single word; we flew into the room as if we were being pursued by Furies??, with fear and with unavoidable passion; we didn't turn on the light; we didn't open the window; we didn't check the cleanliness of the bed linens (it was a 10th-class hotel)!

I felt every muscle of his body as if they were sealed to me, firmly fastened to mine, to my body; my chest, in fact it was a boulder melted down to the softness of wax, our bodies; and nothing, you're not going to believe me on this, M , I felt precisely nothing at that moment, apart from this symbiotic organism, which being double, and therefore his too, was not sufficiently mine. Emptiness! Nothing in between! A man who comes in through me, enters like through a balloon that is alternately inflating and deflating. I'm not in the balloon, nor am I outside of it, nor am I on the back of this lumberjack (like a trailing vine) ... nowhere ... that balloon is something different and not me, that balloon is my swollen viscera but not me!

And I wanted ... on the ship ... on the train ... it ... the body ... to compress his body ... squeeze it..into me ... to absorb him ... and leave him unseparated ... identical with me ... across the lower part of my stomach ... so I render him digested ... completely understandable like the music of Pergolesi ... in my womb M ! Dear M , something is happening with me something in my insides, something through my womb and on up, something on this journey, also, and for the others, travelers, all of that, but all of that which is not me ...

I feel, feel that ferry boat, that dream, that plasma as it collapses into the center of my stomach and a little beyond ... it irritates me like acid!

I'm writing all of this to you in the semi-darkness of a hotel room; the blinds are drawn; My fellow traveler is

asleep, or only pretending to sleep, but that isn't important, nor does it matter that we haven't spoken a single
word; and on and on … M , we're silent! I don't know
his name, or anything about him like in the cabin there
at the beginning; and tomorrow we'll continue our journey, we're only talking through things like food, sleeping,
and tiredness.

A little bit ago, a few minutes ago, I removed a flake
of tobacco from his eye! He washed my back and
rubbed it hard; love M is certainly not what is happening!
However, we are merely loyal (perhaps even devoted)
traveling companions; that is enough, that is quite
enough, M .

the third day?

We slept on the grass near a freeway, in a sleeping bag,
snuggled together; we are traveling with no plan, ran-
domly. And the body—it's not my body, either. Someone
else's … maybe yours, M ? About it (the body) it could
also be said that it is firm, slender, and smooth; however,
it could also be limp and saggy and full of cellulite, and
that would not upset me; so see, it's like it's yours or
Lida's, you remember overweight Lida? With the flabby
body, airy with no snares, unambiguous and clear and
thereby precise as well! Anyway this is Lida's body!

the fourth day

We cruise around this city vulturistically … or like every
house is infected with syphilis. We hole up in the nearby

168

groves and forests; in some abandoned house with a smashed wall or even a missing roof. There's no way we're going into the city. Ordinarily one of the two of us stops a car or a semi, or a refrigerated truck, and that's how we exchange money and at the same time buy our food and beverages. It so happened that one of these men passing by wanted to take me with him with no further ado, without even batting an eye; he showed me his tape deck, in his car, he stroked and patted his leather seats and mumbled something; since I didn't do anything to show I didn't want him to, he, probably thinking that I was on the horns of a dilemma, took out a photograph and shoved it in my face; on the photo only the face was his, from the chin on down the picture was altered to show a body in a speedo; it was one of those guys who competes in "Mister Universe" pageants; this fop held on to the photo super-tight (the last thing in the world we'd want is for those muscles to walk off somewhere) but I moved it to the side just a little and stared at his puny body, if you could only have seen it, M , how simpatico that piddly body; the meaty little package between his sprawling legs covered in the thin fabric of his pants (he was wondrously dressed) and the Hercules bursting out all over, imagine, just imagine it, M, such a life combination! At a moment when I least expected it, the photodoctored lounge lizard slammed his door, grabbed the steering wheel, and the automobile, a far more efficient machine than the one in his underwear, drove in a circle around me once and zoomed off towards the city; and I called after him, that nice man, the one nice man I had met while traveling:

169

Adio amore…and I waved at him, yeah I waved at him and of course I wished him a pleasant trip and the realization of his photographic desires. The next time that I meet him, if I meet him, I'll sit down on his leather seat (the one he so proudly caressed) as if I were sitting on him, soft and slack and warmed by driving and the sun, the roadside sun, convinced that such a crumpled figure, with fake body and the saddest genitals I had ever seen, could change my life…definitively…

fifth day

We decide to change our surroundings…My fellow traveler and I made our way north (so he says, he says it's north, the region into which we were heading), and we had a quarrel…he wanted to go somewhere on the coast, close to the water, he is disgusting; all at once, and then he isn't anymore, and then the next moment he's an asshole again, he's a JERK and he makes me cut his toenails, the swine, it makes me puke, he looks suspiciously at what I'm writing and shakes his head…thank heavens he doesn't understand the first thing and wouldn't even if I wrote in his language, he still wouldn't get it, he's as stupid as you are, M , the two of you would make a splendid pair, I'll introduce you, it's absolutely a must for you to get to know each other…you don't understand any of this either isn't that so and you are just like him

Jelena's Second Letter

sixth day

I'm through with this idiotic letter, but isn't this already day six of my thinking constantly about you and turning only to you, but you, you wouldn't lift a finger, I mean your little toe, to help us see each other! My dumb and dumber M , the dumbest in the world, instead of greetings and similar bull I am going to wrap up this letter in a completely 100% reverse way, against custom, despite our double love, contrary to it, jeering at it, so you know: I send you no regards I have not missed you I am not waiting and I "barely" want to see you

                    that's all
                    for
                    now

CHAPTER FOURTEEN

Mathemetical Symbols for Jelena's Future, or Zoran's Lips

About myself, about Jelena, about Marijana, about the singer Frida, and making mention of completely unknown persons: Circe, Giordano, Fumfos, Stinky, here in the telling of Vladica-photographer, or the strong man in the sign of the fish, or the collegial husband-man of the flutist Jelena, or the Afghani-Nepalese Traveler, an eastern Šumadinian. As he speaks, he smokes incessantly; he boastfully shows off his American cigarettes with eastern tobacco— "Camels"; with his other hand he undoes and then refastens the button imprinted with the symbol "Wrangler" on his grayish-green "Wrangler" jeans. He clenches his arrogant lips, licks his moustache, scratches himself all over his face, he doesn't cough, he doesn't clear his throat, he doesn't belch, and he doesn't forget the significance of his testimony about Jelena. Therefore he also makes no attempt to check it, to confirm it, and to place it somewhere by means of division or multiplication; he's aware that the result or results could be varied or unexpected.

Well … where to start??! I came back, um, yeah, so it was in July, home from the East. That's how they say it, you know, "from the East"—and this seemed totally like the West. But that's a third, or even a fourth story. Belgrade was having its usual wicked heat wave; what could I do besides take a pedagogical approach and get through my head the following one wise aphorism: Vladica, endure, suffer, you had your fill of traveling, though you didn't get your fill of fucking; you took a couple of acid trips, etc., so put up with stinky Belgrade and wait patiently for the flood of chicks, blonde and tanned, to come back from Dubrovnik, read Ayer and write hexagrams or flip through issues of *Modern Photography*, five of them, and memorize them, know them by heart; Nikon Nikon Nikon only Nikon; the Apollo astronauts say it as do I: Nikon only Nikon only only 35 mm, 35 mm, they, and me too, and everybody knows it, ha ha?! So I smile to myself and have a clear game plan for photography and the Dubrovnik returnees. Eh, so what you gonna do? There'll be none of my advice of my autosuggestions (I had recorded a few sentences or was it all just one sentence, yeah, that would be it, on a little EI tape player; in a monotone voice I repeated them several times and played it back to myself, typically at night before going to bed). Things started to fucking suck; the chicks didn't feel like coming home, and August began and I was almost wishing I could travel back to India, even despite that wondrous "sewage system" of theirs and the flies—they devoured my very soul— and generally speaking all their natural activities and organic materials, peace-loving shits, little fingers and holy water, and man I tell you I wanted to go there again but I was scared, I mean, it's normal to be afraid of those diseases of theirs, even with as much as Belgrade, as lonely as lonely can be to an isolated man, and that's me, had become unbearable for me. Well, so then I ran into Marijana telepathically; and everything turned around. I stopped playing the cassette tape with that life message, the July-August one, and I slept a lot more peacefully after Marijana's therapeutic cooking and Marijana's therapeutic breasts. I totally forgot that in July, or rather August, anything other than Marijana's breasts even existed in Belgrade.

At that time I lived alone in my uncle's apartment; my uncle and aunt were already in their second year of work in Austria. And the thing … with Marijana, I explained it pretty neatly to myself, like this: if there's no more Frida … you know, from the group ABBA, then I can have Marijana, right? Share the wealth. And how. Marijana and Frida even looked alike almost. And Frida, she wouldn't be able to resist me. This is as obvious as the sun in July and August … it's clear she wouldn't resist me … oh, Frida. I am marked, conspicuous, striking, right? These hairs in my nose? Oh yeah! That's motivation for a girl like Frida, a babe pure as crystal. In July and August, Marija was at my side every day. In September, she pretty much quit coming over. She'd only visit occasionally, just to, you know, see what I was doing, how I was eating and if I was sleeping peacefully. Would Frida have done the same, maybe? That same way, just sometimes, Sunday afternoon, a strict and mean-hearted rationing. Formula for long-lastingness: being occasional with it! And, hey, my kind of condom—I say mine because I discovered them, what solid reliability … solidly reliable, yeah, like a Nikon, haven't had a single one break, not one single time in July or in August or in September; the hero-condom withstood everything. I should give them a gold medal. I buy them in bulk—the old lady in the corner shop gawks and foams at the mouth. She totally wets herself when I say: "Give me a hundred of them." "Which ones" asks the pissed-off old lady; and she's totally shocked when I reply: "Everybody knows about my brand, Heroes. Hero condoms. Give me a hundred Heroes, please!" Ah … Frida! One should tread lightly, sing (in the bathroom) softly, eat light fare, with no spice, read light literature, and math, have deep and fortifying sleeps—to that end, give up tobacco! So that in September I'll have a stronger brain, my intelligence will become deep, and dispersal, just so you know, Frida, turns into something effortless, no sweat. Frida is my type, my super-type. A moderate masochist, as if she were from the Šumadija, a genuine Serbian woman/Kosovo maiden, and a Swede by birth. Such intuition, Circe and Stinky will turn green with agony, because of this intuition of mine, yep. Even if they exert all the forces available to them, they wouldn't pull it off … They would most certainly never arrive at such a sharp sense of smell for women as I have. Especially for S-types, super-types—I can sniff them out from a distance of 100 meters, easy as pie. I have a special knack for cards—I can tell what cards the super-types are holding in their hearts, as if you had put cathodes on their heads, just like in a scientific experiment; they do everything and do it exactly as I anticipate. I also have particular hexagrams for them. By them I mean the super-types. I simply tell them flat-out, Stinky, Giordano, and Fumfos: "Watch what you do with a super-type. Chicks like that screw with their minds, and definitely not with their snatches." I guess I have like a PhD in parapsychology, wouldn't you say? These things have to be carried out precisely but carefully! But they, those lunatics, they resort to power, muscles and the like. Tactics, it's just tactics! Look, for example, this is something one should know, these types…for instance a M-type, a mucky-type, only screws with a snatch, exclusively. They are total masochists. As for Jelena—what can I say? No way … No, she isn't my type. Not my super-type. Hey, but here a few ambiguities come to light … .She's also for sure not a mucky-type. I would have to think … You see, I don't know right off the bat what to say … Jelena, Jelena … I don't know her well enough, but maybe Jelena is like a J-type for instance. I'm being vague here. I don't know her. A little bit maybe. I know a little bit about her … but what if it isn't the letter "J"—because of her name. What if it's L, or A … .It doesn't matter. Jelena is the pattern for a type like that— J, A, L, and besides, why don't I know what kind of woman she is? She mailed me packages regularly when I was over there … in the East. She didn't write a single letter! I kind of sent her, in return, photographs, of various things. The only thing I wrote, what I would write were the addresses. Well, I could've written a word at least, a few lines from each city even if it was that "dear" and "how are you," and then added my signature but before it "sending you my best" and "love." Something like that. I definitely could have, it's that simple, but I didn't and so, what now?! I didn't do it and that's that!

She wrote to Marijana! Marijana told me that she'd received a letter from Jelena. She said "a queer letter from a queer place." Maybe Marijana's lying! Maybe she didn't get any sort of letter. Jelena never writes; she has never penned letters; Marijana could have imagined that "queer" place and letter. She says, Marijana does, when she undresses, almost—not long ago: "Jelena sent me a letter from Padinska Skela ... from the hospital." I said nothing in return, as I looked at her naked and red with her breasts above my head, more precisely above my nose, my hairs, and I didn't believe a word of it ... Intuition once more! Incidentally, Jelena isn't crazy. She never was crazy, and she definitely isn't right now, there in Padinjak. Crazy, that is. Ugh! Maaaybe she's more of a masochist. I'm not in the clear on anything connected with Marijana?! She came over on Thursday and told me she'd gotten another letter from Jelena, from England, and she said the postmark on the latter, and the stamp were—English; she swore that both letters were credible, since she said that she'd recognize Jelena's handwriting, every bit as much as her own. That Marijana is a complete idiot ... I haven't gotten eyes on a single letter; and fuck it all I know at the very least, I know that Jelena never writes, no letters for anybody; she never writes letters. So I told Marijana that giant retard how stupid she had become, because she doesn' see that Jelena is fucking with us ... with these "queer" letters. This is just like her. What else could it be; thank God that Padinjak and England can't be it, simultaneously, the place where they're from; and how should I know now where Jelena is?! Maybe she's with one of her men, one of her futile screwers, of her friends in low places. She has the most fucked-up way of choosing. I know she liked bow-legged guys with saggy asses like Circe, beady-eyed types like Giordano, and all kinds of heavy-brows right down to monkey look-alikes, where all these flaws congregate in one place. She has probably made further strides in this direction. Or for instance she falls in love with someone's mouth, his ears, the way he walks or makes funny faces, or his eyes, some guy's eyes. Quite idiotic. She has no principle in this, a guiding one. With her eve-rything is a mess. Experiences like that aren't experi-ences. They're not worth the hole in a single Hero con-dom. Take me, for instance; I love only thoroughbreds, I don't like them when they're scrawny or flat as a board. I don't like them if they're bowlegged or have thighs like the trunks of oak trees; in addition I don't love long noses, or thin lips; and also I especially dislike those women whose asses drag the ground; but all the rest, all of the other ones—they'll pass. They don't have to have a face like Frida's or Marijana's or even Jelena's, and it's not a requirement for them to have great big eyes. I'm not splitting hairs here; it doesn't bother me. Now Jelena, you can see how she keeps track of that sort of stuff. Ha. Her heart leads her to eyes. It's ludicrous. Stupid.

As if eyes were important, I mean, how someone uses his eyes; what can Jelena conclude if someone is cross-eyed or blind, what can he see from behind lenses when they're two cm thick? Those are some of her vain imaginings.

Surely from the eyes, actually one's gaze, she, Jelena, is utterly unable to determine if a person loves or doesn't love his or her mother or brother, for example! Maybe that's not the kind of things she thinks about, a mother and a brother; maybe she decides on the basis of the eyes about someone's instincts, life impulses, let's say. Something like that! Maybe?! How should I know?! I don't know what she wanted to prove, what impulse, back when she made me stand on the window-sill on Milaševa Street, at such a height, with a rope around my waist tied to the radiator pipe in the foyer!? I wasn't scared, not me, not then. I have signed up several times for the skydiving club. Now admittedly I've never jumped: no, it's not that I'm scared. It's more that I can't get up at six in the morning; but I passed all the theoretical training; but I did not go out onto the window ledge on the 12th floor, to spite her, for no other reason than to spite her; I wanted to spoil her joy for the simple reason that she was thrilled at the thought of watching a true-blue firefighters' feat, the daredevilish escapade of her husband who is doing it for the love of his wife or to give his wife the first joy she's ever known. I could have done it, I could do it now, too, to give evidence and a demonstration of my will, but there's no need. I am not the tiniest bit afraid. Not then either. I didn't feel dizzy, I mean, I guess I passed, all the tests, my scores were excellent, the jumping prep ... I know darn well that you shouldn't humor women like Jelena, not with a first-responder's feat, with flowers, or tickets to the theater, by making lunch, frequent kisses, nor embraces on the street, loving glances, morning coffee, or breakfast, a little boat ride on the Sava; perhaps only sometimes, by having an intimate conversation and really

really rarely washing her back. Now I didn't say one should treat Jelena crudely, though she does earn her slaps; anyway, I'm not one of those guys who cuts off his womenfolk's ears, noses, hair and leaves little crosses on their cheeks and neck with a penknife. Who could be in a relationship with Jelena? Who could put up with her? Someone might slam her head against the wall in fury, and then serve time for it!

Marijana is a great deal more sober-minded. She kisses austerely and expertly. Marijana really knows how to do it, Jelena rolls her eyes, loses control, and gets scared, pinches and scratches, goes bananas for it and then all of a sudden she's crying, for no reason; and because of that she also makes mistakes when she's messing around on that flute of hers. She quarrels with people she doesn't know; her neighbor from the tenth floor was about to give her a good thrashing when she cussed him out; he chased her practically all the way to the corner of Cvijićeva Street; Jelena must have talked all kinds of crap to him; he's a weirdo, too, a bachelor at sixty. A drunk too, perhaps? But Jelena takes everything too far. She has 17.5 freckles on her face; I didn't count them. She told me that. Maybe she made it up, but her face is truly freckly. Someone should write a report on these reddishyellowish freckles. To wit: the four-year plan for the output of sweat on her face (field: economics), or fear of sunbathing and how to prevent it (field: preventive medicine), or zits and freckles as craters, social craters—the causes of revolution on Saint Jelena or Jelena the Redheaded—fertile ground but underutilized (is that—sociology?)! Of course that uneven number is extremely significant. I'd go so far as to wager my Nikon, plus 500 Hero condoms, that those 17.5 freckles on the face of the woman who is my wife in the eyes of the law, the flutist Jelena Belovuk, everybody's lover, nobody's daughter and the niece of one Maša Pavlović—that number is well justified in parapsychological terms.

I guess people can believe me, since I'm an unofficial doctor of parapsychology, of photography, mathematics, and dispersalism. Anyway, the least trustworthy man in Belgrade—Giordano—believes that all of my nicknames are legitimate and are lock, stock, and barrel—truthful: Dr. Kiss-Kiss (sometimes they also call me "Dr. Love"), and then there's "Dr. Trans-Trans" and "Dr. Para-Para," and people also refer to me as "Tauta," on account of the tautologies with which I vex and oppress everyone who falls into my clutches. This is all true— "Yes my dear everything is trueee," ti-ra-ri ra-ra-ra she says, that is, she hums/chants, she being Lidija Kodrič or some other such starlet-heartbreaker. I always sing that one when I'm in the tub. It goes like: *"yes, my dear, it's all trueee, la la"* and sometimes, you know, like: *"shoobie doobie shoobie boobie moobie shooby yes-yes-yes kiss me and oobie bury me yeah shooboo dooboo shoobie baby put it under the little window—little nettles—booby mooby the little rug ooh uuh yeah yeah Je-lo-looo, yeah, oh yeah, darling of mine, shoobie … "* I belched for two hours without interruption because of Giordano's stupidity, a few days ago! What did he do? He didn't do anything. He had not bedded anybody. But that was the rub, because he was capable of saying: "I'm gonna buy myself a knife this year as a Christmas present." He was distressed and desperate and being as dumb as fuck. He isn't distressed or desperate anymore, but—praise dick!—he hasn't stopped being as stupid as some bubble-butt bimbo. It's not like it's on us, Circe, Fumfos, Stinky, and me, to cure him of his celebrated impotence; it's enough that we diverted him from his suicidal Christmas wishes, and that ... yeah, yeah! What else is there to say? We bugged that miserable Giordano Bruno from 11 in the evening to 4 in the morning. He had to admit that we were right, and amputate his use- less dick and present it to us, embalmed, as a sign of his gratitude, uh-huh, you betcha! Why not? And if we had- n't? I mean we spent that night and the wee hours of that morning pulling him out of the blackest depressive hole, no ditch. And yes, he has to go to Egypt now and study mummification, he has to feel up and examine those pharaohs very thoroughly and it's dangerous, it is, maybe he'll turn into a faggot not because of the phar- aoh but more it's the Eastern wisdom and ancient at- tachment to life. Till the day he dies. Giordano will, foaming at the mouth from excitement, refer to Circe, Fumfos, Stinky, and me as his saviors, He'll never want to admit it but somewhere around the halfway point to the command bridge inside his head, he will be con- fronted with this irrefutable fact. So here is the mind candy and the seasoning from that night and morning and pit of depression in Bruno's soul: we playing *pref* (preference, a card game); the three of us, Circe, Stinky, and I; Giordano and Fumfos are dying of hideous bore- dom; all at once Bruno starts taunting Stinky and Circe, banging on the table, twisting our cards around and say- ing alternately to the pair of them: "What is this, Stinko?

Man … .You're playing *pref*, eh? What in the fucking hell is *pref*? Right, dude? What is it to you, a simple man, this fine game where you are like that flower, your namesake the pelargonium that grows where it lands and isn't choosy, stinky can't be cultivated … .so if you were to lie down on a trash heap before the garbage men came, they wouldn't be able to tell you apart, and they'd shove you under that big wheel that slices and dices everything up, that's the right place for you … c'mon, c'mon, *pref* isn't for you … steer clear of aromatic business like that … drop it drop it … " Then he'd switch to Circe, with no reaction from Stinko, 'coz he didn't give a rat's ass what Bruno was babbling about.

"…And as for you, Circe, you are a dyed-in-the-wool nympho, from your bed to the armoire, and under the bed, out your window, in the toilet on the train to Split, you jerk off non-stop, you don't care where you stick your johnson, and if you can't get it up, you don't even care, you're such a fool that if I showed you the sea, the Adriatic, and told you it was an ocean, you'd think it was an ocean. Your semen has fertilized the universe…You are obsessed and you don't know it…C'mon, c'mon, this is as pointless as your card game, no beating around the bush, no wholesale running from the truth like when you put your puny little worm in the coal chute downstairs in front of the building and you think it was a vagina. You splash around and wash yourself in the sewer and like now you turn off the gray matter or is it white in your pretty little head and dream at night about how you even fuck the stars and Jesus himself, to hell with it, you have a dream about creating a new earth and that

184

titanic trickster Rhea just smiles and whispers into your droopy ear: "Giordano Bruno, world cosmonaut, be careful: in me there is a ton of black earth and a ton of terra rossa...not any sand at all...do your trench-plowing carefully, baby rabbit Brunokins!" Circe didn't even crack a smile, he just laid his cards down and said to Giordano: "That was quite a good recitation but at the end there you were imagining yourself in my place when made a new Rhea and then had sex with the universe, so you see you intended all of it for yourself, and that's why your own name slipped out when Lady Rhea whispered it...Fess up, fess up—how long's it been since you got laid? Out with it, bro, what are you ashamed of...We'll arrange get your pipes cleaned, do you want Jelena or Marijana or that one broad, she's skanky but man she's a brick house...just say the word?!"

Giordano got embarrassed and shut up but in short order he put on his jacket as if he were preparing to leave, and then it seemed like he changed his mind and he took it off again; he stood there over my epic nose hairs, that is, above my schnozz, and started in on me:

"You say, lovingdoctor, that pussy $\neq$ pussy without Hero condoms, right? Your transmathematics goes like this: between me, lovingdoctor No. 1, as a psycho-sociological-physiological-biological-economic-historical individuum and the world, that is, reality in and of itself, that means, objectively, therefore independently of me lovingdoctor No. 1, consequently in the future without me, the relationship is not pure. Because it is mediated; I, Dr. Kiss-Kiss, Trans-Trans, and other things invoking "doctor" status, can only touch reality through a rubber, a thin plastic sheath; the rubbers, officially called condoms, between reality and me are precisely 1,550 in number. That number determines (my) happy efforts at dissemination = the number of good catches from salt water and fresh water = the number of successful fuckings per person, that is, per skirt. My life principle is: nada without Hero condoms. No fartlet (which means you can't break wind). No lifey-wifey (you can't live-work-screw) ... Is that it, brother loving, did I hit on your hidden and wide-open thoughts???"

I don't know what was wrong with him. Really, it looked like he was joking but he exaggerated everything; did he want to mess with our minds? And the part about Christmas and the knife, had he said that intending for us to take it as a joke that he was making at his own expense, but to his benefit we understood it exactly as we should have; then we undertook rescue-related measures; the three of us versus Fumfos turned out to be totally lame, the mother of all good-for-nothings; he ran off. He couldn't bear to watch as we held Giordano Bruno's huge renowned head under the water for five minutes, in the bathtub; he had zero understanding of our salvational mission. We got Giordano good and cooled off with the shower and plunging him in the water and with ice cubes, which we tied onto his nuts and his temples. Thank god he fought it, eh? ... But what can one person do against an intrepid trio of ice-binders and ice-tossers ... When he calmed back down and acquiesced in the injustice of the world order, Circe and I took turns chatting with him about sexual stimuli, sexual objections, and methods of self-actualization in the Middle Ages, other periods, and this century. At 4, before the visit of light-white dawn, Giordano was wet through and through with sweat—his pants were clinging to his butt and his legs, and he was spent from the therapy (only cruel at first glance) but cured and completely happy. Let no one be left wondering: the effectiveness of this kind of psychological method and other similar ones has been verified. I'm not pulling your leg here, not a bit— not a teensy-weensy bit. And the fact that Padinjak, Kovin, and those university loony bins are full, that's for reasons unbeknownst to us, and besides that the therapists are using everything to try to help. I swear by the holy archangel Michael and the real Bruno who got fried at the stake, I started going on about Jelena but have utterly forgotten where I left off because of that wanker, the false Giordano Bruno.

It will come back to me! Slowly! Ah … yes, yes, I was saying something about parapsychology, wasn't it something like that … Whoa, now I know: it was about Jelena's freckles, right you are, about her famous freckles: 17.5 of them on her cheeks, her nose, and a few on her chin. Alas, I know she used to describe men the same way men describe women. Like when we'd get together and talk—which girl what's that chick like does she have nice tits and how's her landing strip; so yeah about Mircea she once said and in his presence too that he had an ass like two peaches.

Those 17.5 freckles of hers, on her face, to be more precise, their main concentration is around her half-pug nose; they're linked to the following things: at 17 and a half years of age, she slept with a man for the first time. He was 27 and a half years old. (She told me this on the second night of our marriage, our friendly one.) At 17 and a half, she learned to swim, to ride a bike, and to roller-skate! At 17 and a half, she says, she loved a guy named Zoran. Simultaneously she fell in love with Andrija. Impossible! So presumptuous! Who was 27 and a half here, and who was 17 and a half? Some nonexistent bodies or Jelena and some real hotshot developed as a PA system?

My official (according to Anđelija's documents) spouse clamored: "It's cracking! It's cracking! The loudspeakers belonged to Boško." I caught her in a lie. She admitted having deliberately created confusion with the names, the swimming, the roller skates, and being in love. And she went on to confirm that she does have 17.5 freckles on her face and claim that some things did really happen to her when she was 17.5. She told me that she loved Zoran's lips and his soft eyes. What crap: soft eyes?! I asked her whether these "soft eyes" belonged to the Zoran from the time she was 17 and a half, or to some other Zoran? And do you know what her response was?! I swear by my Hero condoms and my lifelong trans-position that Jelena uttered these words: "I have no earthly idea what that luscious-lipped man's name was, but I feel like it had to be Zoran." She described his—all right, Zoran's—lips. I cannot begin to tell you how little sense this made to me; other than that his lips were standard; that means they were neither thin nor fat, dark red nor pale pink, not common or rare, neither moist nor dry, etc. And Jelena the maniac says to

all that: "Zoran's lips." Or: "Eh, those lips of Zoran's."
And then, I tell you what, then, it seemed like all of a
sudden to me, it dawned on me like the sun over
Pancevo that that phrase "Zoran's lips"—that was his
total definition. Precise, accurate, the definition of
Jelena's ghastly infatuation. Likewise it subsequently became obvious to me that this was in fact a ruse of hers.
The tactic of a fallen woman. I confirmed that the
phrase "Zoran's lips" doesn't serve here as the expression for one of her states of blazing fucking. I established, also, that this famous Belovukian sentence does
not exist: " A touch between Zoran's lips and mine, pol-
luted air, an insurmountable journey." The truth is: I
don't know what actually happened to the phantasmagoric somnambulist Jelena-body the censer and Zoran the
luscious-lipped, the eloquent, blue-eyed yessir by god
blue-eyed just like the sleepwalker Belovuk. No one informed me of this. Not even the prompt spy, my con-
frere Circe; and even Mircea—known in bed as Eli-
ade—not even via his petite left ear has he heard the
faintest peep about this earth-quaking liaison: "Zoran's
lips" = Jelena's forehead with its skin-omega when she
gets angry, when she talks earnestly, and most seriously
of all when she curses my mother. But I know, unmis-
takably and definitively, that Jelena will eventually, if she
has not done so already, implicate Zoran. She will pull
him with her and we'll be presented with the crude
mathematical equation: $J=Z$. I can't foretell how; but I
feel with a sixth sense everything that's going to take
place. Since Jelena is insatiable, she wants Sancho Panza
and Quixote at the same time for half an hour like a

double bid in *pref*, and when all her desires are fulfilled, the following occurs: J ≠ Z. J ⌐ Z. And so on in turn. For example: Z ⇒ (∞ J) or J ⇒ (∞ Z). Zoran implies infinity in Jelena or infinite Jelena (these are not identical). And possibly vice-versa.

I drew a butterfly on the collar of her shirt, one of her shirts, before I went away on my trip. One fine day like any other, she will grow to hate Zoran; and in mathematics and in his and her life that will be a disjuncture or alternation. The exclusion of a third. Luscious-lipped Zoran—a third element. It will be enchanting to see this.

But where is Jelena actually?

I would go so far as to swear, and moreover that's something I never do, swear by priests that are red, purple, green, yellow and, look, the same color as my Levi's shirt, blue; by the cross, star, triangle; by the censer and my mother's first communion at St. Nikola's, and also by the editor of the I-TV station (he promised to hire me) that Jelena Belovuk is not in Padinjak, but despite the stamp on the envelop from Great Britain, she also isn't in England. She doesn't speak a word of English.

Last Wednesday I went to see Jelena's aunt, Maša Pavlović. I helped her move, as did Marijana. She was changing apartments. It would appear that Maša, the widow of Anton Pavlović, was again getting married. The late Anton isn't giving her trouble anymore. But the living Jelena never reaches out. Maša Pavlović is convinced that Jelena will come back from out there, from the clear blue sky and the great big world, "with a bun in the oven." She says she's forgiven her for everything,

and for everything else till the end of her life and whatever she's just about to do now. In advance. If only
she'd welcome a child, her own child, Jelena's. In the
end she threw me out of her house because I said to her:
"Aunt Maša, you're still pretty sturdy, not to mention
fertile, so why don't you have a child and grandchild
yourself?"

*

The sober and knowledgeable Marijana disappeared
somewhere. I don't see her anymore! In this cramped
city and despite Circe's snooping around and Mircea's
intercessions, I cannot find her!

*

My current girlfriend has tits down to her belly button,
and kneesocks pulled all the way up like two loaves of
dark pink bread, ready for parapsychological baking =
oven at a distance of 100 km. She gets upset easily. Clas-
sic M-type. I miss Jelena. My official and sole wife.
Wife-child.

*

And Aunt Maša sighed, that day, and whispered: "Jel-
kica-fir, aunty's aroma, parfumerie, my darling, gorgeous
little apple."

*

I am still prepared to assert: Jelena has sequestered herself somewhere with Zoran the Luscious-lipped. She just
won him over; he fell hopelessly in love. He buys her
chocolate and wine, washes the dishes, makes bechamel
sauce for the boiled beef, scrubs her back every night,
scratches her belly and the soles of her feet, straightens
the bedding and pours the semen into the bathtub.

Guaranteed, a hundred percent, that's how it works. Where's Jelena? With Zoran, naturally. Check it out if you don't believe me! He lives in one of those small houses in Sremcica!

*

But I have to go now. My parapsychological oven awaits. I can sense that it has warmed up and is red-hot ... !

CHAPTER FIFTEEN

Jelena's First Letter

———————

Marijana ... are you listening right at this moment ... to the *Missa Luba*? Imagine:
a huge building, not all that white, a sanatorium for people with nervous breakdowns, located on Avala or in Padinska Skela ... it doesn't matter ... where. Marijana! Along the narrow corridor, which is precisely four meters long, with pictures on the walls, and the doctors say that these pictures are "neutral," pictures of landscapes without a single human figure, along there walks a tall, bony woman with a dusty, worn-out hospital coat over her shoulders, locks of her slovenly red hair falling down her big like whips; she smokes incessantly, that woman ... Marijana! I am still not sure if that woman was Ksenija or if maybe that woman ... was me?

... in the hospital cafeteria (first door on the left) the tv is on ... That means, however, that the date cannot be 1955 ... At that time televisions were rare, and only a few people had them ... Important people ... After all, lunatic asylums surely weren't thinking (do madhouses think? That joint "I" of doctors, benevolent nurses, and snaggle-toothed housekeeping staff) about entertainment for crazy people (=those idiots who didn't belong to the joint-associated "I" of physicians, nurses, and cleaners), but it also would not have been in accordance with that: "neutral"; and so all of that, the voice of the announcer, the short excerpt from a ballet performance, the deafening applause ... must have been twenty years later ...

the thousand hands of a crowd of ballet lovers and ... of lovers of art in general, actually, Marijana, in 1955 ... does that mean that the same ballet troupe was on stage twenty years earlier ... I've forgotten their names—it was some kind of French name ... It will come to me, it will ... the announcer was talking about how these ballet dancers from France were visiting some municipal government offices and institutions ... and Skadarlija, too, and some notable personages, or anyway who they walked all around and called attention to themselves on the streets of Belgrade ... .those French visitors, the ballet dancers ...

still, Marijana, I am not completely convinced that the red-haired woman in the narrow corridor of the asylum where the "neutral" pictures are all over the walls isn't Ksenija ... she is clapping but isn't listening to the *Missa Luba*; the mass is just rattling around in my head, in dribs and drabs; that *Missa Luba* is on roller skates, cruising across my left spongy-tangly slime thing. My brain.

i have zero sense for music ... i'll take a hatchet to my inner flute

she, Ksenija, is applauding for that ballet from 1955 ...

in 1955, on the second day of the visiting troupe's performances, they, the members of the corps de ballet, are being shepherded around to schools and theaters, and Ksenija, whose relatives and husband, father, mother, and some of her friends called Senka or Senja, and she who gave her child, the first one she had, the name Senka although it had hydrocephaly and died quickly, she really was just a shadow in that narrow four-meter long hallway at the sanatorium on Avala; then, when the ballet dancers, on point (by habit), walked around Belgrade and were entering, and exiting, and entering the specially spiffed up, scrubbed down, and decked out educational institutions (for this occasion) she was already the dead Ksenija ... Do you understand, Marijana ... in insane asylums there weren't any televisions back then ... probably.

It's likely that the ballet ensemble departed the next, that is, the third, day ... went back ... by plane ... to Paris ... .probably ...

whose hand flipped through the papers, on that day, pedantically copied out as they were with stamps, signatures, and a diagnosis ... was that hand shaking, Marijana; at that time, that year, I was 28 months old ... Exactly 29 years and a couple of months was how old Ksenija Belovuk, nee Olvin, was when her death erased the last reason for ...

no, I am not Didona, that Didona who used to shout exoriare aliquis nostris ex ossibus ultor ... after so much time it's as if I am talking about someone else, but in actuality her death did erase the final reason for me ever to shriek with the violence of a Didona ... If it ever occurred to me to do that, it was in high school do you remember Marijana when that monster Jelić that dwarf of a professor demanded at the meeting of the teachers' council that I be expelled from school because "I was a bad influence on the other pupils" on account of my short skirts, and my underwear that you could see when I sat down, my make-up, how I made out and smoked in the courtyard, the bathroom, the hallways, and for my suggestive giggling, you remember Marijana, you also wore short skirts … and your legs were even longer but they didn't throw you out, you weren't a "case" in a lyceum as famous as our Fifth; and it could not have happened to you: to lose the right to an education because you had not learned by rote two poems each by Rakić Dućić, Santić … and that is exactly what happened to me; you were every bit as brilliant … but you were not afraid in the least of saying to those idiots Marićka and Jelić, in front of all the other teachers and ten students, do you remember it then, Marijana, you were just exactly like Didona: "You are all shoemakers. Your job is cutting up raw, tough hides … freshly butchered ones, and then in your cobblers' workshops in the breaks you read glorious Serbian poets and peek up the skirts of the customers." And you said something else, I think you swore at them, and you said they were fascists even though they had party cards of a different color; and after that there was a real uprising in that august lyceum, but you didn't give a shit, and all they could do, that whole bunch of pervs that they were, was piss in the wind, because you already had your diploma in your hands. I always shared your opinion. I always thought that the teachers were reeking piles of shit, crown jewels of stench, glories of the pedagogy of masturbation, of beating their meat, and the eyes of the German instructor always ended up under the desks and on the knees of the female students, so Marijana, I always thought like you did, but I never said anything, not even to that midget Jelić.

Marijana, my dear, time is not measured here by devices but by the whiteness on the walls, according to the patterns on the metal tables and high metal bed-frames, by glints on the glass, gleams on the bars, so that's why I never know for sure what time of day it is ... the damn fluorescent lights are on almost all the time. We scratch out little sketches, cut out symbols, carve things into the metal ... the dealings of the delusional ... the walls are always whiter at some point before dawn ... I've established ... that the others are crazy ... I was brought here by the will of two types of lunatics ... brought in ... from outside ... from inside ... "noose-ready," they call it ... they say that, and they know best, they tell you that, Marijana ... I've got bruises on my wrists from the ropes ... that was on the first day, and the second ... they've stopped doing that, but it's weird, because the bruises seem to be expanding according to some scientific law, spreading, turning my brain matter blue. Bruise-brain. My brain is a bruise.

So maybe my condition could actually be evaluated. What do you think, Marijana? I don't know exactly what's wrong with me. It's not like having some problem with your flute. It's true that I don't know, and the doctors do. The intense stench of the beds, the brass, the room, the nurses who scratch us with their long red fingernails, red ones, they hop around, in the doctors' rooms they settle down onto their tiny pricks, and the ceiling comes crashing down along with somebody's brain. The ceiling is always caving in … whenever the nurses walk through the rooms, the corridors, any-where in the asylum … the doctors' cocks have good distance vision … the nurses smile sometimes. Their fingernails are grubby. They drink coffee, specialized vocational-school training, but nevertheless they are crazy, the erection at home isn't enough, nor the one at work, on the bus, on the Pančevo Bridge, on summer vacation in Orebić, their hair is falling out, on all of them, clumps in the sea, the bus, the pipes at home, everything's clogged with the hairs from their heads, medical science and smelly vaginas, specialized voca-tional-school training … but the flute—what do you think, Marijana?

They don't give me electric shocks; there's no need to rouse me to instant life. After the electricity comes emp-tiness, amnesia—and it's easy for crazy people to think they're the doctors, in a moment like that—therefore those other lunatics, the other breed that has "doctor" on their clothes, don't like the electricity; anyhow didn't they use electricity later on, trying to shove life back into Ksenija's body; for all they cared, Ksenija could turn into a vampire, because of that electricity, life bolts back in and all of a sudden, boom—but the doctors? Those limp-dicks. They lived for the rear ends of donkeys, oxen, and the parking lot attendants … and as to whether I am now Jelena Belovuk or Ksenija Belovuk, they don't wonder about that at all, they leave me to what the nurses say are my "hallucinations," they're still saying I'm a liar, these female students of medicine, they say I am imagining that I have bruises.

And the milligrams: 100, 50, 25, three times a day, chemistry for better digestion. They smile then they give it to me, this pharma, and they say it will help me, these people with the word "doctor" sometimes shout, open their little eyes all wide and stuff and raise their ... eyebrows, their lab coats jump out at you, and their ties, but their shoelaces are undone. And you, Marijana, will be the first to say, and I know it, I know you, you'll say this: "she's strange, that Jelena that is to say, Ksenija."

I'm tossing all the medicine into the toilet bowl ... they still haven't caught me at it, and they want to increase my chemical assistance, and they tie me up sometimes, and, tsk tsk, after that famous high school, and the famous music academy, and the famous city, and these famous people—there's the famous lunatic asylum Padinjak. I'm falling into glory. And my brain-bruise! The brain is a bruise jammed into the glory of buildings, musical-educational-madhouse buildings. The straitjacket of Ksenija Olvin. You probably mean pyjamas, you say, but Marijana, where'd the mortar in her clenched hands come from, and around her breasts, in her rubber slippers, between the fourth and little toes on both feet, and in her pocket, the lime, crumbles, actually little pieces of mortar, plaster, and you say, all right fine, but from where, where's the mortar from that's in my hand, Marijana, where's it from when your brain is a purplish black bruise. Powdery plaster in my hand. I have red hair, and I haven't colored it. It's red, and you can see the mortar, and under that it's purple. The bruise. And those shitheads lunatics medial trainees without the "doctor" on their white clothes, they say, it's always the same thing, see, they say it, they tell me I'm lying about: the Bruise.

Listen, Marijana, what do you care about these things from the asylum, send me bananas, two kilos, in fact you could get me five, that's a lucky number, mine, and then also bring face cream, for me, you know the one, the one I use, and OB tampons, those bitches with the red fingernails give us each five grams of cotton, a scrap, chocolate, some bars of Nestle's, big ones, and ham and cheese, buy that cheese from the open-air market, toilet paper, I promise not to asphyxiate myself, don't worry, they keep tabs on that here. Water. There's no way to bathe when you want to, but you know when they smell bad, the nurselings, with the red nails, at home they take baths on Saturdays and holidays …

Marijana, time does not exist. Eternal life. Eternal woman. Saturday rituals. State holidays. If someone would touch me … if someone would touch me, I'm not sure jesus mary and joseph if I exist … I am still not certain that I exist, with these cords, this Ksenija Belovuk in me, this is Ksenija in me and she's arguing with somebody, it looks like she is explaining something to someone, that Ksenija, under electric shocks, but nevertheless nothing exists actually except for SANATORIUM SHITTING AND PISSING ON THE BEDS ON THE POLISHED FLOORS Ksenija breaks her neck, the others laugh but they also break their necks, the floors are slippery. In the bathroom at Padinska Skela one is accompanied by a nursling, she laughs too, she has a separate area for herself, for her red brain and her read nails, she has no butt. I'm going to trip her with my outstretched leg, that is with my bruise, with my head so that she busts hers, there in the bathroom, my bruise in the rubber sandal, my leg, I'll kick her ...

But, someone has to come and get me out of here, someone no matter who, Marijana, somebody has to come immediately. Now, Marijana. Now.

Ksenija is talking with someone. She says, she Ksenija Olvin Belovuk that time is aspic. Fatty.

They, here, don't give anyone a bedpan. They think that we're crazy that we could pee on our beds, through the bars. I feel sorry for them. I cover up with my vomit-stained yellow-red-orange-green-brown-olive drab-purple blanket. Imagine an asylum having multi-colored blankets. My hospital coat has no buttons. They gave me men's pyjamas, in their haste they also almost assigned me to the men's ward, the room and unit next door, at Avala. You can't close the fly on the pyjamas, and the upper part has no buttons. Every-thing's open. The ones who ogle when they pat me down, the doctors, those doctors have patent-leather fasteners on their uniforms. Time squats here. It's cold around my head, bring me a toboggan, the one that I knitted. My bruise looks like an amoeba, I need a warm cap, and don't forget by the way pencils, I want to true, I have to draw, they told me, this squatting thing. Who are the cords for. Since time has been squatting, my whole head has been freezing, after sleep it's like an icicle, I finger it I don't sense it, although I know that it has swollen and the blue has extended even further. But I am not completely a bruise, I don't know what portion of me is, there is no mirror, it seems to me that it's the majority of my head. I don't see it. There is no mirror. Whose arms await?

They took us with a separate, special bus, a bus expressly for special people. Do you know from where? From Guberavac. There we were all sleeping in one room … fifty of us associated lunatics, some of us associates went outside to pee, in the courtyard, passing us racing by were people, buses, close by, in the morning around eight, the driver yawned, cursed and yawned again, called us "crazy motherfuckers," I tried to explain to him that that was a mistake, this bus was a mistake and him being in it, but Ksenija Belovuk did not know him, the driver, she never saw that bus. He cursed, the orderly held me with both his hands, he was a mistake too, perhaps even the first one.

People will be saying these things, Marijana, you will be the one that talks, my double, my traitor, you will betray your very self:

" … *The doorman at the Hotel Central told me that there, in their hotel, a woman arrived, on Saturday, dressed lightly, a girl, upset, before dawn, day was just about to break when she got there. They gave her a room on the second floor. She came down several times requesting him, the doorman, to be sure to wake her up if there should be any calls for her, on the telephone. The porter says that at seven she came back and made several calls, he says she was dialing one number, with no response, he says that she snapped and ground up a cigarette between her fingers ... as she was calling, several times, he said. Afterwards she returned to her room, the porter explained to me, he swear by his only son that he was telling the truth, that some people came sometime around eight, in white outfits, coats, hospital orderlies probably, something like that, and they led her away, tied up, he said she was wrapped and bound, that's how he put it, with ropes, he says that she, the woman, had red hair, bags under her eyes, a small bosom like a girl and that she was crying, that's what he said, he said that it seemed to him that she was crying, that she was resisting and that the men were pulling her along like a filly ... and that all of a sudden she calmed down and left ... as if by her own volition ... but in their hands ... that's how the doorman related it, and also that they took her out the side exit, onto Preradović Street."*

No one is going to believe you, Marijana! No one will believe you that everything you're going to talk about happened in this day and age. The ones who know best are going to tell you that this could have happened twenty years ago, but today? Absolutely not ... Something along these lines is utterly impossible, with force, ropes, the Hotel Central, and the side entrance at Preradović Street, maybe in like 1955, but not today, not in this city, nowadays! That's how the intelligent ones will talk, and the even more intelligent ones will tell you that over there in Russia or also in America those things with rope and whatnot can happen ... but here?! Well, twenty years have passed, even more, they're going to say to you, and for twenty years we've been building roads and other stuff, and things like that don't exist anymore, ropes, bars, vomit-stained sheets, pyjamas without buttons in a ward for the mentally ill. Will you agree with them, my dear Marijana?! Maybe the Hotel Central in Zemun should denote a particular place in my head, something special. I mean, should I Ksenija Olvin make an invisible map of the hotel, the hotel rooms, the whole turn of events with little embroidery needles, those Chinese ones, in the convolutions of my brain, and then make a xerox of it … Machines like that probably exist, cameras, beaming down from the sky, they can probably capture invisible documents in our brains!

If however this is 1955, then it's her head that's out of whack, hers, not mine, and what am I doing here? My issue is that I feel like a hermaphrodite and not like a contemporary woman. The doctors' eyes scream, the nurselings', on the x-ray, they are cracking jokes, evidently, the in-in-interior of the female, look here, nurse, cover up this glaring nakedness, doctor, asks the nurse medicine-woman, what does this 'in te interiore' mean and could it be something different, could we argue on our backs on this machine, making love, I think, as the machine records, registers, documents. Brain. Bruise.

Aureole. I have the aureole of a female saint. A naked female saint. My body is crazy white. It's not mine. They think my body is white and clean in point of fact it's anemic but it also isn't mine. I was thinking about Ksenija while she lasciviously entered my body and then became it completely … I didn't say anything to her about it. Twenty years ago. I also didn't mention to her that the 20th-year entry caused me a great deal of pain, pushing her way into my pores, penetrating my walls and cells, and that since then my grey matter had become a bruise, and begun to run. The bruise is going to kill me. Ksenija has drowned in the diluted mass of my secretions. What can I say to her after that? I should turn my skin inside out. They gave me an enema, and then bitter salts. They investigated my insides. I killed myself. Chemistry returned me shoooved me into something that was blue and gleaming. I feel I am here. But where has Ksenija gotten to? Why the hell has she ceased applauding for the French ballet dancers; there goes the announcer, stating again: Janine Charrat, famous ballerina, and the announcer says nothing about how much she's already done and danced, how many years, and then: Hélène Traïline, René Bon, Jan Bernard Lemon, then the news is over, and they're saying tomorrow the temperatures will be even lower, and snowdrifts, snowdrifts, for heaven's sake—the ballet dancers! Such artists, Janine and Rene and Helene and Bernard … how will they get through, and how will the plane take off? I don't understand … but why did Olvin stop clapping … was it because her hands were holding plaster, mortar, little chunks of wall she'd broken off … and how did her hands cramp up.

Janine Charrat and her friends sent kisses and enormous smiles … and it was so cold, biting cold, people love ballet in the year 19—the insignificant Ksenija Belovuk, abruptly ceased being a lover of the ballet … lover … lover of my body … wanton … hung up, do you understand Marijana why did they afterwards move the "neutral" pictures from the wall and put up new ones, toothy Janines and Hélènes smiling geographically like that all the way to Paris … and they locked up that room with the plaster in my hands, that room with the wall that was dug into … by my … by Ksenija's hands … a little while ago so long ago … it feels like so much time has passed … but actually just a few moments … a little bit ago the newscast ended on television …

a weight on the covered floor of the dining hall of the insane asylum Avala Padinjak scorched and fabricated in my stretched brain I'm going to vomit to Nozinan Nozinan let these lunatics with their "dr." labels give their little ones injections of Nozinan I feel I'm choking they forced me to drink it they threw me into the third world a middle world … not mad not sane … a hybrid type obtained by the application of Nozinan.

Nozinanian nowhereland.

Nowhere, nowhere, nowhere are there creatures like these—Nozinian is the 10th wonder of the world such progress … my god! Nozinan imparted plurality unto the world. Ah, these creatures are neither mad nor sane but compound! You can get them to straighten up, and clean their rear ends if necessary, they'll agree to it gladly, well nigh enthusiastically … you only have to tell them it's for their own good, for their health, and you know yourself that they'll believe you unconditionally.

Marijana, it's good for you to know: to those who have succeeded in making hybrid creatures, this sublime, for real, indeterminacy, the professors at the medical school will send over a medallion and letter of recognition. And thanks be to God Almighty … such a success: to make (just like that, easy as pie) good-natured creatures co-existent with the rusting metal of the beds in Padinska Skela, on Avala. And all you have to do is: swallow one hundred mg of Nozinan daily.

When they give it to rats, Nozinan, I think they'd be able to wean them away from stealing eggs and scurrying down hallways and they could teach them that it's the most suitable thing in the world to snore, squat, stroll a little bit and then squat some more, the rats would squat (thank God and Nozinan) and maybe just maybe all they would emit would be sounds, neither Eastern nor Western, neutral ones, sounds that would influence growth, or the height of future generations of Nozinian rats ... and so forth Marijana ...

Ha! At least the world would be rid of one of its troubles! And those who didn't go along with it when the Nozinan was tried out on them (precious Nozinanian capsules, consumed in vain) can make the beds around here, and as a reward from time to time the creators of Nozinan will permit them to make coffee and enjoy close relations with the red-fingernailed medicine women.

Who can grasp that in the heads of this third world, the heads ... in the heads of lunatics, hybridized creatures actually, dreams have the same meanings, not symbolic in the least, as in the daytime, when one does not sleep, as in the daytime, when we take little strolls down long narrow corridors; we sit in the dining hall, which is wide and long, a space if you will for hybrid creations, not forgotten, and on our walks, by day, we peek into the bathroom, into the doctors' offices to see if anything's up, whether letters have arrived, packages, did anything happen in the bathroom such as a flood, or: one of the rednailed nurses slipped and broke her left arm, her hand that hand with which she poked needles like an executioner into fatty flesh ... not on me ... not on me, but something similar, very important, the same meanings: the moon is a moon, an amputated arm is an amputated arm, and so forth. Freud is of no help to them here, nor is anyone else of his ilk, for I tell you what Marijana, if you dream that your arm is gone below the elbow, then it's truly gone, if you dream of bell tinkling then it's truly there.

And they tie us up from time to time despite Freud and the rest ... someday they will have to disclose that secret ... what's the trick ... what's up with the ropey-rope, they'll have to tell us about that, too, at least in the moment of death ... A rope, really?

I should enroll in the piano department at the academy, or in the conducting program. Flute, shmute! Marijana, don't forget the face cream, the ham, bananas, and paper!

There is no fear; the neck of the hybrid creature is so thick there's no rope that can stretch around it, clench it—Nozinan creates a greasy thick substratum ...

They only succeeded in deceiving me a few times. I drank the magical "medicine" and dreamt that I got new teeth, not false ones, or rather that new teeth grew in. I became a fan, and fast ... I watched soccer matches on TV, and back then, I understood none of it ... but who competes by pushing a ball past things, brains in four languages ... How do they really ... have a bad accent? Anyhow, it doesn't matter, do you understand, Marijana ... Now I throw every little pill into the toilet ... Do you want my head to get bunged up with that? Twenty years ago? Now. It is always now. The bruise is now, too. She must have been asking incessantly: now, shouldn't that be done now?

Thinned breath, in my nostrils I feel my heartbeat, that's just a small break in my attention. I concentrate. A twenty-year question ... breathing. My diaphragm has quieted down. Marijana, it looks like you're pouting—no need! Why are you staring at my eyebrows! They're moving? So that's just a pantomime. And the stain on the wall?! I know everything. And the gouged wall (not too much) and the gypsum in my hands, fine then the mortar, have it your way, okay it's mortar there in Ksenija's clenched hands. Her elongated neck but they say there was no rope, they say it was something else from the doorframe hung my body. A dead dog croaked at the doorpost. Inattentive mistress of the house. Negligent hospital staff twenty years ago, but now. So boring, she is that, Ksenija Olvin Belovuk, with her whispers ... forever whispering something ... Out of that hole in the wall, the tiny hole ... What use is it to her if I'm a mummy. I expose my eyes. Nozinan.

The grounds from a cup of coffee, there, in the doctor's quarters, like mud from a spa; the nurselings don't suffer from rheumatism, their necks are strong, their nails, too. Group calisthenics: the hybrids eject breath, and insert it, breath – freight, that is breathe in, breathe in yet again, like this: the letters W-H-U, as if you were whistling or puffing out into cold air, like this ... Hybrids are worthless. What was that about your attentiveness?

HYBRIDS FROM AVALA HYBRIDS FROM PADINJAK the year 1955 one must keep track of dates! I didn't get the chance to meet the famous Janine Charrat, but I sent her a telegram: how and why? Well so because one can only clap at a ballet like that, clap to stay clapped, and Hélène Traini and everyone in the troupe were fantastic, in the hallway there on Avala that was four meters long, here, with "neutral" pictures on the walls, with the grates, those are good because of the math involved, and the winter ... and the snowdrifts ... and the airplane ... it made it airborne at the last moment ... and the families ... theirs, there ... who were languishing in the waiting rooms ... and landing en pointe, the plane on the tips of its toes, do you get it Marijana, just like that, it came down en pointe ... My gratitude, I said in the telegram to Ms. Charrat, my thanks, I said, and my respects and the rest of it, for Ms. Charrat and you Ms. Traine and you Mr. Bon and of course you too Jan Bernard Lemon, you walked on the tips of your toes like the airplane, you simply snuck around while I bit the dust suspended in the doorframe, a dog would at least have whined, that's obvious, dogs are very noisy, they whistle and puff no doubt in cold weather on Avala, dogs bark and rage, and ... and ... damned if I know what all else. What all else, but you Helene and you Rene and you Jan and you dammit Danijel, Ms. Janine, you all excel at everything, you peep through (how many keyholes) into the four-meter long corridor and wonder why Ksenija Belovuk, why I, stopped applauding ... and once more en pointe like the airplane that departed on the third day on the tips of its wheels, to Paris I guess, you get lost in the woods on Avala, in the filthy streams, there were drifts, but they were soft and soggy ones at Padinska Skela, on the bridge to Pančevo you kept asking around on among the passers-by, why hadn't they already taken down the body from the door jamb, that dead dog stuck in the doorframe, that woman who'd croaked, about whom you'd known for ages that she was a lover of ballet. So, you weren't capable of doing anything, that's clear, you rushed off to the airport, onto a plane that was completely balletic.

She, Ksenija Belovuk, is whispering something to me again; she has grown so horribly thin, as if she were a ballerina. I didn't tell her anything about the telegram addressed to the troupe with Janine Charrat. Of course. I told her nothing….but she's being a bother and inquiring about people and humming some tune. She's standing on the tips of her toes on the edge of the hole in the wall. Avala. The Avala crematorium. Cremating all noises in the hole in the wall, but leaving the hole untouched. How stupid! It isn't even a hole. It's just a little fissure … Ksenija is waving her hand. What happened to it, well fine, with the mortar I mean … what became of the mortar, and her dress … I believe they took out the plaster mortar … did they get rid of it?

Perhaps in the particles a tiny thread of the dress was left behind?

While she's whispering to me, waving her hand and being annoying, and nevertheless being annoying, Ksenija Belovuk is wearing a white (rain) coat with shiny leather closures on the pockets; dark thick nylon stockings, and over them dark gray (it seems like they were knit) socks: black flat like men's shoes, with thick soles, and laces. She keeps her hands in her pockets: there's no smile; her shirt, you can see beneath the jacket, is unbuttoned; her hair is covering her ears; her eyebrows are straight, narrow on the ends, a bit thicker in the middle. I can't see whether her lips are also straight. By the way, I also can't see mine, but I know they are, my lips, straight. I don't see the plaster ... I don't see the crumbles of it ... but the crack is readily visible, and so is she! And it's the same: the Avala crematorium or the crematorium at Padinska Skela. The only that that isn't clear is who's going, afterwards, later, when all the letters are unsealed, the surety arrangements, the will, and the others, who's going to pay the debts. And they can't find the plaster. But they gave permission for the crematorium. Anyway, don't tell them, Marijana, I deluded them, there are no special reasons here. Her decision and mine and vice-versa, understand! The crack in the wall should be closed up yet again and all reasons for crematoria rescinded; it seems like I am annoying myself, but she Ksenija, she's also bothering me, out of that crack constantly, I turned my back on her let her do what she will, I'm going to bed, I'm not interested in ... that plaster. The plaster on her body.

THERE ARE REASONS FOR ALL DEBTS: by your hand, Marijana, with the movement used to kill a fly, usually people use a book; pressure is applied with a book, all at once, abruptly, sneakily, it's a matter of grand strategy: the stain on the wall is all that's left of the blow-fly, the only thing that remains as a receipt of that motion;

the object (book) with which not all too much pressure is applied (to the wall) and the hand that held the book: testis unus testis nullus. The smudge is wiped away. The heavy zipping around of the fly lasted an hour, maybe two; it's unbearable, and there's no debate about it, to listen to the hysterical flight of the fly in a room with closed windows. How did the fly even get in?

That question is also not essential ... Anyway, how it got in there, the fly, whose business is that! If it's already here then it should be released from its hysteria. Who gets released? The room or the fly? That's also not the question, at least no one's asking it out loud, at least we're not asking loudly, Marijana! The fly should simply be squished with one stroke, fast, before it escapes, before it makes its way into a crack in the wall!

If everything is already done, there's no need at all to keep asking questions, and to be astonished, and to assert: the blowfly buzzed an hour long or two in the room where the windows were closed, it didn't flee it had nowhere to go, it got smushed by one almost balletic movement against the wall, the stain was wiped away, there's no witness, that one, that is nobody, a book brought together treasonously with someone's hand; they took an oath to one another, the book (presser) and the hand (mover), to maintain silence; the secret must remain undiscovered somewhere between the hand and the book ... The echo of the aimless agitation of the crushed fly in the room scarcely lasted a few seconds; some people said that was enough for the inertia for that motion to be repeated in the head of the person whose hand pressed the book to the wall. Anyway the echo of the fly's humming, don't you see Marijana, stays in the room where the windows are closed, however frightfully brief it is, although the stain is painstakingly expunged … one must take care not to damage the freshly whitewashed wall …

> January, twenty years ago
> or now, now for real
> Love,
> Jelena

(From the pen of Jelena's biographer)

Epilogue

A t the same time as Jelena I too was wondering about sudden life and sudden death. But I was making no attempt whatsoever to investigate whether she actually ended up in the asylum in Padinska Skela, or in the sanatorium on Avala; or even if she's in England, somewhere in England! There are moments when I accept the sober thinking of her friendly husband Vladica; he believes Jelena's having a laugh at our expense, joking with everyone except Zoran, in whose apartment she's holed up! Let no one reproach me for indolence or lack of interest in Belovuk, because there's none of that to be found in my decision (nevertheless) to investigate no further. I've grown frightened!

Sometimes such irregularities and deviations from precise sequencing are possible in cosmic events; scholars and nonscholars, laypeople and busybodies, skeptics and believers, unbelievers and others, in this context, wrangle over the "instantaneous parapsychological configuration of the senses." All of this leaves me thinking about the riddle, and not the solution, about Jelena's presence in the lunatic asylum and in England—"twenty years ago but also now" –as she said.

From the center of the world the comment of scrupulous logicians:

"That last sentence is meaningless."

But here's where the trouble comes: to refute that sentence is an equally pointless chore.

Anyway, nobody should ask me: Where is Jelena Belovuk?!

I give you my word of honor that I don't know.

Afterword

A Nozinanian Nowhereland:
When (Auto)Biography Becomes
Topography

Introduction

Mountains are supposed to guide us. Don't they, tradi-
tionally, frame and give form, play host, to our activities
and perspectives? We rhapsodize them, climb them,
stack forts and towers on them, bomb them, photograph them, try to stick labels and boundaries on their
flanks and passes, and tunnel into them for all kinds of
reasons. The mountains in this novel are certainly important—one of them especially. That main one, Mt.
Avala, a real place just south of metropolitan Belgrade,
is so important that it overshadows the very title of this
bracing book.

Avala is the specter haunting this novel, but there are
others here, too. A Chilean visitor to the capital brings
the whiff of the Andes; a perpetual university student
blows off Europe for the Himalayas. The meeting of an
outdoor sports society that Jelena, our protagonist,
plunges into total chaos includes large numbers of male
mountaineering enthusiasts, while vacation haunts along

the Dalmatian coast feature cliffs, boulders, and peaks. And a woman compares her love to a massive Balkan mountain range.

The mountain of the title is a storied place, with hints of ancient and classical habitation and spiritual importance. It is a big, beautiful, forest-cloaked mountain, often present in folk songs, legends, and epics from Roman times through the anti-Ottoman rebellions and into our time. A nationalist stratum of significance is added to the mountain when we consider the references to it in Chetnik songs from the last century, and the NATO bombing of its giant television tower just before the current century began. The Serbian tomb to the unknown soldier is there, designed by a Croat (Yugoslav) and built in the 1930s. Most of the mountain is a national park, it's wildly popular for outdoor recreation and picnics, and—there is a sanatorium there.

For Avala to fall—well, a lot needs to happen. And the fall will set a lot of other things in train, we can bet. What could cause this mountain to fall?

About the Author

Biljana Jovanović (1953–1996) was a remarkable figure in the history of late Yugoslavia. She was an innovative novelist who wrote prose of enormous power. She was also a vigorous and conscientious human rights activist, first in post-Tito Yugoslavia and then in the Serbia of Slobodan Milošević. She was born in Belgrade, took a degree in philosophy, and lived for parts of her adult life in Ljubljana. Her parents, both from Montenegro, were prominent communists.

The family had, and maintained, strong connections to Montenegro, which was a constituent republic, or state, in the various Yugoslavias from 1918 to 2006. Montenegro had a separate political history from Serbia, where Jovanović was born and lived and worked; it was a kingdom prior to World War I and is today again an independent state. But multi-ethnic Montenegro, encompassing both charming coastal towns and rugged mountains of legendary grandeur, is intimately connected to Serbia by culture, language, and genealogy. Indeed, Jovanović's fiction is shot through with Montenegrin characters, memories, and other associations. Indeed, her first two novels contain numerous autobiographical elements.

Jovanović's civil society work commenced in the early 1980s in organizations working to promote discussion about issues as varied as freedom of speech, the death penalty, and environmental protections, and it culminated with the Civil Resistance Movement during the Serb-Bosnian War (1992–1995). She organized expressions of solidarity for Bosnia and demonstrations, including of the type we might call "happenings" or, today, "pop-up protests." She published open letters and polemics, taught at underground schools and seminars, and wrote and staged plays aimed at heading off the spread of ethnic nationalism and violence as Yugoslavia was dismantled. She traveled by whatever means she could among the growing number of Yugoslav successor states in the 1990s, collaborating with friends and artists and intellectuals from all the republics, putting forth concrete proposals (such as simultaneous citizenship in all the new countries) aimed at giving citizens options in an increasingly authoritarian and militarized Western Balkans.

Although most Serbs today know her name—and there are reissues of her works and a street named after her in the capital, Belgrade—and also know that she was both an activist and an accomplished literary artist, one often still hears the description of her as an "enfant terrible" or "cult novelist." These epithets are not wrong, but of course they are incomplete. Jovanović represented both culture and counter-culture; she produced four plays, three novels, two anthologies of correspondence, political sketches and manifestos, and a book of poetry, all of which are worthy of continued study and circulation, while working as an editor at a major literary journal and committing herself unsparingly to alternative politics and social change. Interest in Jovanović's writing, both on its own terms and as a manifestation of or spur to her ethical engagements, has remained strong since her untimely death. And this interest is growing. The National Theater of Serbia recently put on a dramatization of the anti-war letters of the small group of women writers of which Biljana was a part, and a collected edition of her plays and selected prose was published by Women in Black in Belgrade. She continues to be prominent in feminist scholarship, both in publications (see Bibliography below) and at conferences.

Had "Biljana" (as Serbs often refer to her) lived another decade or so, we would doubtless have a much richer public archive, on YouTube for instance, of her countenance and voice, in action, with many other courageous women and men, and among friends, witnessing for peace silently and eloquently, and arguing and presenting and, I imagine, pleading and grieving. As it is, we know how highly her peers thought of her, as for instance, in the appreciation penned by Borka Pavićević cited below. We know how enduring the effects of her novels have been, and how much integrity and authenticity she brought to her work in various domains. The novel at hand, *Avala Is Falling*, was published in 1978 and was her breakout success. It, like her second novel, *Dogs and Others*, which already exists in English translation, is a runaway train of a reading experience. Although Jovanović was active in many genres, *Avala Is Falling* might be the ideal introduction to her work or her world. It is unexpected; wildly ambitious; taxing; both polyphonic and polymorphous (and, some might say, self-referential and intertextual); quietly, surprisingly meticulous; sometimes hilarious; and, ultimately, breathtaking and rewarding.

Summary: Into the Whirlwind, Or, A Belgrade Diary with Sex and Meds

This novel lumbers through the life of a young university student in Belgrade named Jelena Belovuk. She studies flute at the Academy, a state conservatory, although aside from a few mentions of instruction, rehearsal, and concert appearances, we would barely know it. References to culture, high and popular, abound, as do mentions of cultural institutions, associations, and infrastructure. Jelena's life in Belgrade is subdivided, or demarcated, by several axes: chronological, erotic, and spatial (her living situation for instance, with Marijana, by herself, with Vladica, and with Aunt Maša).

The narrator for the bulk of the book is Jelena herself. Other guiding voices include her anonymous would-be male lover (the "biographer"—who might actually be [some facet of] her) with his hand on several chapters; the "Lookout," an anonymous observer and creeper of, again, arguable provenance; Marin, a conductor; Vladica, the "collegial" husband; and, possibly, Jelena's fictitious "Siamese twin."

Readers will immediately notice the difficulty of the text. It is highly…irregular. One can call it willful, defamiliarizing, experimental, and all of these things are true in terms of punctuation, syntax, and diction. But the language of the novel is rich and, perhaps surprisingly to first-time readers of Jovanović, very well conceived. It is as carefully thought out as her comparisons and plot lines are, ultimately, consistent and conscientious. In addition there are alliterations and assonances all over the place that point us to puns and bits of poetry. If we are open to it, there is humor, and lust, and, in the original, great fun with adverbs; *tutorski, delfinski,* and *lešinarski* are hard to translate indeed, because "like a tutor" and "dolphinishly" do not do much for us. If, however, we take the last of these morsels as "vulturistically," we can perhaps enjoy a bit of the marbling in her delicious prose. Other of Jovanović's innovations are less quirky than eerie, as in the plethora of words and phrases she employs convey the notions of watching and being watched, often from the side or as an instance of doubling.

Many of the characters appear in the novel as Jelena's sexual partners. All but one, Marijana, are male. All but one, Bautista von Schouwen, are products of Jovanović's imagination; the Chilean was a real historical figure, although he died before the time of the novel. Jelena's other lovers include: Mr. Swede the Mustache; Vladica, the peripatetic perpetual student; Mica, an army officer in training; Petar Martinović, the secretary of her apartment building's tenants' council; Vladimir Ristić, a sketchy chess player; Martin, her conductor; and probably Sale, a waiter.

The novel is set in Belgrade and environs (Novi Beograd, Mt. Avala, Zemun, Padinska Skela, Surčin), with one sequence, described in "Jelena's Second Letter," somewhere in Western Europe. This is for sure in a ferry boat crossing the English Channel; a few other hitchhiking scenes are hard to pin down. There are also references to coastal Montenegro and Croatia, to Chile, and to mountainous South Asia. As in both of her other published novels, there are many very specific references to streets, buildings, restaurants, and other places in the city of Belgrade. Many observers have noted this "assemblage" but there is little agreement on how to interpret it. In the eyes of this historian, these topographical realia serve a function similar to "enumeration" in the works of other writers. It does help to document an era or way of life that is passing, but it also anchors the text in plausibility and verisimilitude. The Yugoslav context is vintage Jovanović, in part because she can be viewed, as I have argued elsewhere, as a sectarian leftist whose views reflect the evolution of Yugoslav socialism after the anti-fascist struggle of World War II. But in the case of the myriad locations in the translated novels and also in the untranslated *Duša, jedinica moja* from 1984, the living nomenclature serves to tame, or domesticate, the phantasmagoria of the happenings and the narration of the book. This is real, the café and street names are saying; the lights of the concert hall and the destination boards on the buses want us to see them and think—these things are nightmarish but the author is not delusional. It is all real. In a way, perhaps the Belgrade-ness of Jovanovic's work is the opposite of the "magic" in magic realism: the wondrous (barbarous) strangeness is already there, and so why not these normal, quotidian things?

The plot unfolds as a series of reports on the life of the student, Jelena. They are mostly thoughts, memories, and conversations, with action and events made apparent indirectly, in flashbacks or through verbal description. The reports, or reportings, if you will, are provided by Jelena and her friends, lovers, and observers (stalkers, actually); above all they deal with her amorous and social relationships. In addition to her lovers, the characters include Jelena's Aunt Maša; her late uncle Anton; Ljubica, a young neighbor; Bosa, a sympathetic neighbor; Anđeljia, a government clerk; Professor Radić; and a handful of characters from the sports association.

Many of the fifteen chapters zero in on one of Jelena's relationships. There are numerous internal monologues, but also outright digressions, some of them hefty. References to psychological illness and mental health institutions abound. Jelena is dissatisfied with her relationships with men, some of which are violent; she yearns tempestuously for Marijana, who is at one time a rival and a muse, a dear friend and a moving target; her aunt, from the redoubt of family seniority and apartment ownership, cuts her to the quick often but is herself a pitiable figure; two of Jelena's lovers in particular, Mr. Swede the Mustache and her "husband of convenience," Vladica, are particularly nauseating losers. Ultimately the plot hinges on scattered attempts to answer one question for the reader: what happened to Ms. Belovuk? After rolling through these months in the Yugoslav capital, in the (indirectly dated) mid-to-late 1970s, Jelena either goes to England and off of our radar; is murdered in greater Belgrade; is hiding out with one of her lovers, also in greater Belgrade; or dies in a hateful, pharma-soaked sanatorium, probably the same one where she experiences phantasmagoric dream sequences, or delusions, or is even transformed into her mother who met a disastrous end there in the 1950s.

**About This Book, or The Weird People
One Meets on the Way to the Catastrophe**

There are always multiple ways to read a novel, just as there are multiple Jelenas, and multiple angles and takes on any given Jelena, in this particular novel. Feminist interpretations of *Avala Is Falling* have been the most numerous and enduring. They have been effectively elaborated and rely on sound psychological insights and consonance with Jovanovic's activism, which was, however, distinctly polyvalent. Feminist interpretations have tended to focus on the role of the protagonist's body and the effects on her psychological state and actions the disappearance of her mother in an asylum; readings in this vein also naturally highlight gender inequality, harassment of and violence against women, and discrimination. Other critics have focused on the book as an example of "jeans prose," or an effort to problematize the generation gap in East European cities. This term was popularized in a 1976 study by the Croatian literary scholar Aleksander Flaker, who took inspiration from contemporary writers as varied as J.D. Salinger (US), Vassily Aksyonov (USSR), Ulrich Plenzdorf (East Germany), and Françoise Sagan (France). This has also proven to be an enduring label for Jovanović's work, and it is not as simplistic (or condescending) as it might sound today, because this generational paradigm involved major shifts in language and novel structure, a prioritizing of sex over sentimentality, and a sensibility for cinema, rebellion, and "anti-bureaucratic attitudes" in general.

There are other, less common interpretations that are bracing to consider. There would be, for instance, a certain logic in construing the book in philosophical terms. The characters often weigh in on issues of ontology, perception, and free will embodied in characters whose names are often drawn from classical thought and literature. For example, the Serbian literary scholar Tijana

Matijević pointed out to the translator that "Kirka" from Chapter 14 is a reference to Circe from *The Odyssey*, while the very uncommon word Jovanović uses in key passages for "someone who loves or craves" is the same one used in Serbian translations of Platonic dialogues. One might consider *Avala Is Falling* a kind of spectral mystery or an intellectual whodunit, or, at a stretch, a kind of modified modern "road story." In very much a different approach, Matijević states in her forthcoming article on Jovanović that the novel is vastly important in its Yugoslav setting and context because it manifests the potent revolutionary intent to move beyond women's emancipation to a "liberation of consciousness"; that is, the novel is both singular (about Yugoslavia) and transformative (stressing intersectional potential).

The translator might here be able to add to the mix a different historical reading of this novel. Two elements in Jovanović's writing here really jump out at the reader: the cultural infrastructure and the global register for comparisons and a frame of reference. The first term refers to the cultural references, especially musical ideas, composers and works, institutions, etc., that are so abundant in the novel. The second term denotes the international content of the book: from the Chilean revolution to camping in England, from French ballet dancers to Italian fashion, from American horoscopes to tourism in Melbourne, and beyond. What might be the intention, or the function, of such references, of one category or even together? My understanding of the joint effect of the inclusion of these two categories of elements proceeds from acceptance of the novel as a kind of fictional historiography. The intertextuality, self-referentiality, and epistemological anxiety of the mediated, even hostile, manuscript glower poignantly out at us from the beginning of Chapter 12:

> The other things, which have been the subject of fatuous statements by cravers and ravers, and Jelena's actual and potential lovers, believing that they're participation in the global ordering of wisdom—I have rifled through and amended those; dates, for instance, and places; I've limited their characters and unlimited Jelena Belovuk….

But Jovanović's novel does not contain or imply simply a postmodern view of history. The cultural and cosmopolitan infrastructure rescue it from that. They point to an unconventional approach to place and time, because we have a geography based not just on motion or stasis, or on Yugoslav or non-Yugoslav, but on inside and outside as defined by gender. Males are privileged in Jelena's world, and they cause enormous suffering; women are less powerful, to the point of being not only contingent but even fitful, episodic, in their presence, including to themselves. (Witness Jelena's Siamese twin.) But the world, because it is accepted by both genders, and both sides in the Cold War—indeed, there are a few Cold War references in the novel—is outside, permanently and effectively outside. Music, and high culture, manifested in buildings and sheet music and educational institutions and cassette tapes and television shows, is also "outside." In a novel centered on a self-conscious woman character, the counterweight to contingency must be theorized in the presence of some kind of outside. Even if it is aspirational, this outsideness allows for a dynamic portrayal of the city of Belgrade as both real, in its material and male aspects, and realized, for its female characters. This innovation might be termed a historiography of inclusion.

Conclusion

It is sometimes remarked that this book launched Biljana Jovanović as a writer, but that it was in her second book, *Dogs and Others*, published two years later, in 1980, that she truly found her artistic voice. That may or may not be true. The second novel does indeed take the reader apart with surgical precision, or with a well-aimed burst of machine-gun fire at the heart, while *Avala Is Falling* lurches and sways and attacks fitfully with whatever blunt instrument or body part is at hand. Still, Jovanović's first novel is, arguably, a more ambitious work than the second one. Her target here is all of society, not just a (fictionalized) family. Everything from the system of higher education to courthouse marriage requirements to airport sub-cultures to hitchhiking culture to communal life in a major housing complex is fair game. And Jelena's sexuality, like her person, ranges over a vast amount of territory in *Avala*, presenting us with everything from wild escapades to dreariness to date rape to humor to jealousy to "friends with benefits"; in *Dogs*, Lidija suffers from rape, sexual assault, harassment, discrimination, infections, drug abuse, and more—and even her female lover tries to crush her. There is a decided difference in tone and scope. Meanwhile, *Avala* has already given way to the tidal wave of challenges to form and style, and it very much clears the path for the explicit portrayal of the love between two women in the later novel.

Both novels have at their hearts a furious attack on concepts of physical and mental illness and the delivery of care to citizens who are ill. And both present extended, painful takes on urban family life. There are no happy endings here. Jelena Belovuk, for her part, might be spinning her wheels or being dragged down, but the world around her is moving. Neither option, stasis or change, as depicted here, seems good for her. Or us.

John K. Cox
(History, North Dakota State University, Fargo, ND)

Bibliography

Flaker, Aleksandar. *Proza u trapericama: prilog izgradnji modela prozne formacije na građi suvremenih književnosti srednjo- i istočnoevropske regije.* Zagreb: SNL, 1976.

Hawkesworth, Celia. *Voices in the Shadows: Women and Verbal Art in Serbia and Bosnia.* Budapest – New York: Central European University Press, 2000.

Jovanović, Biljana. *Dogs and Others.* Translated by John K. Cox. London: Istros Books, 2018.

Lukić, Jasmina. "Svemu nasuprot (Energija ženske pubune), in Radmila Lazić and Miloš Urošević, eds., *Biljana Jovanovic: Buntovnica s razlogom* (Belgrade: Žene u crnom, 2016), pp. 17–33.

Matijević, Tijana. "Biljana Jovanović, a Rebel with a Cause: or, On 'a General Revision of Your Possibilities.'" Forthcoming in *Wagadu: A Journal of Transnational Women's and Gender Studies*, c. 2020, available at: sites.cortland.edu/wagadu.

Pavićević, Borka. "My Soul, My One and Only." Translated by John K. Cox. Published at www.pescanik.net on August 7, 2019.